smoke and gravity

smoke and gravity

by Win Neagle

The Paper Journey Press

The Paper Journey Press Book Club Edition, January 2005

Copyright © 2001, 2005 by Win Neagle.
The Paper Journey Press Book Club Edition
First Published by The Paper Journey Press, 2001

All rights reserved. Printed in the United States of America.

No part of this book may be reproduced or transmitted in any form
or by any means, electronic or mechanical, including photocopying,
recording, or by any information storage and retrieval system,
without written permission from the publisher.

This is a work of fiction. All names, characters, places and incidents
are products of the author's imagination or are used fictitiously.
No reference to any real person is intended,
nor should it be inferred.

We gratefully acknowledge Nick Boland.

The Paper Journey Press: http://thepaperjourney.com

Cover and Book Design by: Frank B. Powell, III and Sharlene Baker

Library of Congress Card Number: 00-110145

International Standard Book Number (ISBN)
0-9701726-0-5

Dedication

For Rebecca,
without whom neither book
nor author
would be complete

introduction

I go along with the wise readers who feel a little put off when they encounter an introduction, by a different writer, to a first novel. Surely if the story is any good, we think, it will stand on its own handsome hind legs, needing neither ornament nor special pleading.

But every now and then there appears a work of such startling originality, a voice of such distinctive timbre, an outlook so keenly quizzical that it deserves some sort of encomium that might help to attract notice. I feel that Win Neagle's wildly funny, wildly fleering, covertly serious *Smoke and Gravity* is one of those highly infrequent productions. What a breath of tipsy oxygen this novel is! One might call it "Voltairean," or "maybe a little bit like Kurt Vonnegut," but these comparisons, though they might entice, are inaccurate. This book is original.

I won't make any predictions about the future career of the author. My crystal ball went cloudy in 1958 and has remained so since. That was the year Mary Ann Dobbinson turned me down for the date I had fantasized about for the previous six weeks. But I do feel safe in predicting that if you enjoy zany, knowing, whimsical, and utterly untrammeled humor, you will like *Smoke and Gravity*.

I suppose I ought to admit that ever since Mary Ann said No my life has been just a shade dimmer than I'd hoped it would. Maybe that's why I'm so grateful for this book: Laughter can lighten, for some happy while, even the most rueful of long-agos.

And laugh I did. My wife, who detests hearing about Mary Ann, was alarmed at the noise I made.

—Fred Chappell

Our indiscretion sometime serves us well
When our deep plots do pall, and that should learn us
There's a divinity that shapes our ends,
Rough-hew them how we will—

>Hamlet, Act V, Scene ii
>—William Shakespeare

>"Where most of us end up
>there is no way of knowing,
>but the hell-bent get
>where they are going."
>
>—James Thurber

To say Myron Fugate stands naked in his backyard may not be completely accurate.

He is, indeed, in his backyard, a vast expanse of land as backyards go. Between Myron and the rear boundary of his property rest nearly thirty acres of rolling meadow and an occasional tree.

However, it might be more accurate to say Myron Fugate throws boomerangs in his backyard. Scattered within a twenty-pace radius of Myron lie forty-nine of his seventy-five boomerangs, and at this moment he is reaching into a cotton laundry bag to select the v-shaped projectile with which he will perform his fiftieth toss of the evening.

Or maybe we should reconsider the word *naked*, for though it is true that Myron wears neither shirt nor pants, *naked* might conjure up an image of complete nudity and might give an impression of slight, perhaps even total, vulnerability, and it is difficult to picture Myron Fugate as a vulnerable man.

Myron tosses his fiftieth boomerang of the evening. It is one of his cheaper, plastic boomerangs, but its flight proves true. Holding steady to its elliptical flight pattern, the boomerang pretends to zoom past its nearly naked thrower, but then stalls in a hover, allowing Myron to reach out and gently pluck it from the air. It is the sixth catch he's made this evening. Myron tosses the boomerang aside and gives himself a congratulatory stroke of his beard.

The beard is one of the elements that renders Myron *nearly* naked, rather than completely so. The beard is longer and grayer than one might expect for a man under forty years old. If he were to stand straight and tall — which is unlikely given Myron's preference for a casual slouch — the longest of the coarse, gray strands might stretch from chin to navel when pulled taut.

Besides the beard, Myron also wears a tool belt and a pair of brown leather work boots.

It should be kept in mind that except for overhead air traffic on its way to and from the airport in nearby Charlotte, it is highly unlikely that while in his backyard Myron will be seen by any human other than his girlfriend, Bambi, who is inside the small, three-room house Myron built with his own hands more than a decade ago. Bambi is in the living/sleeping room struggling to work the kinks out of her latest invention which we will discuss in a few moments.

Myron's workboots are of a pragmatic nature. Most weather conditions suitable for lawn mowing are also suitable for boomerang tossing. Therefore, Myron seldomly mows his monstrous yard. The boots are protection from any stray glass or nails that might be lurking beneath the knee-high grass.

As for the tool belt, it should be apparent that the presence of large obstacles is not conducive to the sport of boomeranging. And since a table would surely qualify as a large obstacle, if one wanted to have an evening cocktail or two in the same vicinity as one throwing boomerangs, one (the one wishing to drink cocktails) would be forced to hold all supplies in his arms.

And what if one wished to be both the boomerang thrower and the cocktail consumer? This is the question Myron posed to Bambi several years ago, and though Bambi's specialty is inventing exercise equipment, not drinking apparatuses, it took less than a week for her to arrive at a simple solution. She had Myron take her to Home Warehouse, where she purchased a tool belt that was easily customized to hold a sixteen-ounce bottle of Coke and a pint of bourbon.

Using a soldering iron, she then attached a money clip—an old silver one she'd bought at an auction and had been saving for Myron's birthday—to a tin cup she found in the back of Myron's lone kitchen cabinet. The cup clips securely to the belt, and though there's an occasional slosh, it's not as if a refill isn't handy.

A Quick Note about Pickett, North Carolina

The word "suburb" tends to bring to mind a dependent relationship, a collection of homes occupied by people who depend on a nearby city for their existence. It is important to many of the residents of Pickett — Myron Fugate, for one — that the world is aware that Pickett has not budged in over a century, and it is Charlotte that has grown toward them, making itself an uninvited neighbor.

In a house located in one of those neighborhoods of Pickett which endanger the town with the label "suburb," one of those mass-produced neighborhoods of nearly identical homes, all priced in what many in Pickett can only fathom as make-believe dollars, Ted Rumpkin III sits at his computer playing Pac-Man. Ever since the death of his dental practice, Ted Rumpkin III has spent many hours at his computer playing Pac-Man.

His wife Sissy sits across the room on the sofa, knitting a blanket that has been in progress for nearly a year, yet remains smaller than a potholder. Tonight she is knitting even more slowly than usual, her mind filled with thoughts of their London vacation, the beginning of which now lies barely twelve hours away.

She can't knit, thinks Ted Rumpkin III to himself. She can't knit, she can't sew...can't cook, she's a boring conversationalist, but she does have one true talent... spending our money.

Yet Ted Rumpkin III knows his wife Sissy won't be spending their money much longer. For soon, they will have none.

Seven years ago, Ted Rumpkin removed the wisdom teeth of Linda Coxdale. Prior to and during the procedure, Linda was administered nitrous oxide. As far as Ted Rumpkin III can trust his memory, the operation went per usual. But once the laughing gas was cut off, an enormous glitch appeared.

"You awful man," declared Linda Coxdale. (This actually came out "oo-awv-oolan" due to the Novocain, which had numbed Linda's lips and tongue.) She then stormed out of the office without paying her bill.

Later, in court, Linda would accuse Ted Rumpkin III of fondling her breasts — which happened to be of the small and firm variety, ideal for lounging braless in T-shirt and jeans — while she was under the influence of the nitrous oxide. Then a psychologist from Charlotte proved to the jury, and perhaps Ted Rumpkin as well, that, no, the defendant was not lying, at least not intentionally, when he testified he had no recall of "caressing, fondling, poking, or touching in any manner" the breasts of Linda Coxdale. No, according to the psychologist, the truth was simply not available to him, for Ted Rumpkin's above-average mental faculties had done a top-notch job of repressing the memory, burying it so deep that the truth might never have popped up again were it not for the just-minded citizens of Pickett who would certainly not let such an injustice go unpunished.

Linda Coxdale's attorneys then spent two entire days proving that, just as the psychological expert had stated, Ted Rumpkin III did, in fact, possess "above average mental faculties."

In the end, the jury granted an award of seven hundred seventy-five thousand dollars, plus an additional two thousand dollars for reimbursement of Linda Coxdale's dental bills over the previous ten years.

Ted Rumpkin III realized the damage was even more severe than he had imagined when he returned to his office the following Monday to find it empty. No patients. No hygienist. No receptionist. Not even a picture of the children of the receptionist.

Ever since, the once prominent dentist has paid a monthly lease to Clyde Austin's used car lot to ensure there are at least three cars parked outside of the office at all times.

Once, while waiting in the check-out line at the grocery store, a jovial old farmer commented, "That guy with the '72 Camaro sure must have some rotten teeth."

And now the last grains of the Rumpkins' savings are preparing to slip through the hourglass. The upcoming London vacation will take them close to zero, maybe a little below, especially if Sissy finds space left on any of the credit cards.

"We have to cancel the vacation," Ted hears himself say.

"Excuse me, dear?"

"London. We've got to cancel."

"Why don't be ridiculous," says Sissy, tossing her knitting to the floor and turning to face her husband. "What about the neighbors?"

"The neighbors? I guess they can go to London if they'd like."

Sissy Rumpkin stares at her husband, wondering if he's always been an idiot or if the stress of the breast scandal has eaten away at his brain. "I mean, what will they think, dear? Surely they've noticed we haven't traveled for over a year. Not even once. I'm not sure, but I believe there may even be a clause in our homeowner's agreement concerning non-travel. With all of our problems, do you really want to risk losing the house?"

We're losing the house, thinks Ted Rumpkin III. It's only a matter of time. "No, it's just not feasible. We must cancel." He utters this statement with confidence, as if he believes the matter to be settled. But underneath the authoritative tone, he knows the fight has just begun.

Cecil Leadman moves from mailbox to mailbox with a bag of thumbtacks and two hundred fliers for Bert's Mowing Service. "Call Bert, He'll Cut Your Grass. 248-1714."

As he attaches a flier to the last mailbox in the exclusive Timber Haven subdivision, his attention is drawn by the hysterical shriek of a female voice. Upon closer examination, he deciphers the situation to be this: A woman is chasing a man around the yard cupping her breasts and uttering the following phrase, or close variations of it, over and over, "We need money, Teddy boy?! Huh?! Huh?! I said, DO WE NEED MONEY? THEN JUST GRAB THESE! We'll be rich again in no time."

The couple circles the house three times, and then the man flees back into the house. The woman continues her breast chant and makes two more laps around the house before the man opens the door and begs her to come inside.

Cecil tacks a flier beneath the couple's mailbox and calls it a day.

A Note Regarding Cecil Leadman's Mailbox Fliers

"248" is not, nor ever has been, a telephone exchange in Pickett or in any town nearby.

In the course of his life, Cecil Leadman has run across three people named Bert, none of whom has ever mowed lawns professionally.

And if a Bert in Pickett did cut grass, he would almost certainly refer to himself in the first person on his homemade fliers: "Call Bert, *I'll* cut your grass."

Scratching a mosquito bite on his naked hip, Myron clings to the dusk as if it were the last drop in his bourbon bottle. The only remnants of sun are stray rays that have scurried from below the horizon as the sun turned its back, smacked their heads against the industrial clouds of Charlotte, and now stumble punch-drunk into Myron's meadow.

Thirty years ago a stranger told Myron that dusk was like an open window where all souls, living and dead, could dance together to the last song of the day. The man had come to Myron's Little League baseball practice and afterwards asked if the two of them might speak for a few moments.

"I knew your father," the man said as they walked toward centerfield while the rest of Myron's teammates were piling into their parents' station wagons and pick-up trucks.

The words filled Myron with a warm chill as if the man had said he'd once shaken hands with God.

"I met your father the day you were born," the man said, causing Myron's chill to grow darker. His father had died of a heart attack only hours after Myron's birth. "I only knew your father for a few hours, but sometimes that's long enough to know most of what's important about a person," he said.

Myron and the man faced the pines which were beginning to mask the sun.

"By the way, my name's Stan Noffsinger. I'm not sure it was such a good idea for me to have come here, but I think of your father a lot. He made a big impression on me. My daughter was born the same day you were and it's impossible sometimes not to wonder about you as I watch her. The day she took her first steps I wondered if you were walking, that sort of thing. Earlier I talked to your mother and told her something she thought I should tell you, too."

Myron looked up at the man, still not finding words, but wanting him to go on.

"You may not have ever met your father, but you

filled him with joy. The hours before he died, he was one of the happiest men I have ever seen. I just thought you should know that."

A silence followed until Stan attributed to Myron's father something he had always wanted to believe. "One of the things he told me the night he died, the day you were born, was that at dusk you can speak to anyone, past or present. It's nature's window to eternity."

Myron stared into the fading light. "I guess I should be getting home now. I'm glad you came by."

As the two walked towards Stan Noffsinger's car, Myron turned once more to the diminishing sun. "I like that you were happy, Father," he said softly, and then he shuddered with delight as he was certain he heard his father answer, "Just remember this: things will usually work out if you let them."

Back in the present, Myron tosses his four-foot-wide "Kango Monster" which cuts through the darkness and ends its long flight abruptly against Myron's unsuspecting skull. Myron lets out a burst of laughter and capitulates to the night.

"Goodnight, Father. Goodnight, Mom."

Inside, Myron finds Bambi suspended from the ceiling by two large, black strands of rubber. This is the prototype for her latest invention, The Dangler, a home jogging device. Though not certain about the specifics of how one might utilize The Dangler in a personal fitness program, Myron's quite certain that if he removes his tool belt, and then removes Bambi's nylon shorts, and then retrieves the short wooden stool from the kitchen and positions it under his dangling girlfriend, the two of them might have some pretty good fun.

He does these things, and the fun far exceeds "pretty good."

At the Rumpkin residence there are no rubber bands hanging from the ceiling. But there is sex. It is sex of the shameless prostitutional variety. Sissy Rumpkin straddles an anonymous cock, riding with all the enthusiasm she can muster in hopes of bringing things to a quick end, whereas the owner of the cock, her husband Ted Three, is hoping the sex lasts indefinitely, for he knows it is going to cost him money he does not have.

Sex is also present in Cecil Leadman's small, absolutely spotless apartment. Cecil works an average of

smoke and gravity

only three days per month and spends the rest of his time cleaning his apartment.

At the moment, he sits on the toilet in his tiny bathroom, distracting himself by recalling the breast chant performed by the recipient of his final flyer as his bowels struggle to empty themselves. The door is open, which is not irrelevant, since being closed in a room with his very own shit could easily initiate Cecil's death, or at the very least, a nervous breakdown.

There are no lights on in the apartment. From the television a few errant rays have found their way to the bathroom, behaving in much the same fashion as those sun rays that struggled earlier into Myron Fugate's backyard. The television rays bounce from a black, polished table over to the only other piece of furniture in the apartment, a white plastic deck chair. It is plastic because Cecil abhors padded furniture, holding against it the difficulty, if not impossibility, of trying to render it sterile.

From the plastic chair the rays play pinball off of the three framed Ansel Adams prints that anchor the living room's spotless walls, make a quick tour through the closet-sized kitchen where they strike Cecil's only dinner plate which sits clean in its tray in the stainless steel sink, waiting to be washed once more before being put into use.

From the plate the rays find their way out of the kitchen and finally to the bathroom where they are absorbed by Cecil Leadman's large pupils.

Most people might absorb such a minute quantity of rays without noticing. After all, only a spattering of rays have made the journey from television to pupil. But for Cecil Leadman the rays are almost blinding.

And what about the sex in Cecil's apartment? At the moment, the sex is primarily confined within the television, but the escaping rays have acted like sperm, carrying the sex from the muted television that displays the pornographic video Cecil rented earlier in the day and scattering it throughout the apartment.

Cecil is painfully aware that after he wipes himself he must face another physical necessity of his life. He is thankful that he is capable of limiting this other messy activity to a semi-weekly basis.

Cecil walks to the kitchen like a condemned prisoner. In the cabinet beneath the sink a battalion of soaps and cleaners stand at attention, and off their right flank is stationed a small stack of brand new hand towels. Cecil removes the top towel, walks calmly into the living area, spreads the towel between his coffee table and deck chair, inhales deeply, and takes a seat.

The photonic lovers do not stop to notice him, the male working away diligently in an attempt to please the two women with whom he shares the screen.

Cecil forces himself to concentrate, wanting the

ordeal to be over as soon as possible. The television remains muted, the trio moaning away in silence.

With a roar, Myron plunges backwards off the stool, landing next to his tool belt on the worn carpet. With a smile on her face, Bambi bends to kiss him, but the oversized rubber bands run out of stretch and snap her towards the ceiling.

In the Rumpkin bed, a soon-to-be-repossessed French reproduction, Ted Rumpkin lets the last undepressed part of his soul exit his body in a defeated grunt.

Sissy Rumpkin dismounts and begins to pack her suitcase.

The TV flickering before him, Cecil Leadman allows himself a quick and quiet gasp, then hurriedly refastens the fly of his slacks (which now need ironing, he notices), grabs a corner of the towel between thumb and forefinger, and with outstretched arm he marches to the kitchen where he deposits the towel in the trash pail and shuts the lid tightly.

"I'll wake up early and take the dogs in," Sissy tells Ted.

"Okay…great," he mutters.

"I'll need some money."

"How much?"

"Well, it's kind of expensive, but Olivia's Canine Bed and Breakfast is one of the top kennels in the country."

"How expensive?"

"Not that expensive…one-twenty-five."

"For the week?"

"Per night."

"Per night! Goddammit, Sissy! How in the hell can 'not that expensive' translate to one-twenty-five per night?"

"Each."

"Each what?"

"One-twenty-five per night…for each dog."

"That's it. I'm doing what I should have done all along. I'm canceling the trip," Ted Rumpkin says, making his way to the telephone.

With a leap, Sissy Rumpkin straddles her husband much as she had earlier in the bedroom.

"Give me the phone. I'll call my brother."

"And what, have him beat me up? Shoot me?"

"No, you idiot, I'll see if he can keep the dogs."

Ted Rumpkin's depression leaks through the surface of his anger and leads him to surrender. "Okay. If he can keep the dogs, we'll go to London."

Once again, Sissy Rumpkin dismounts in triumph.

Any true dog person will have noticed that the Rumpkins are not true dog people. In the preceding dialogue, their two beautiful Irish Setters, Stonewall and Lee, were not referred to by their given names a single time. No true dog person refers to his or her dog as "the dog."

Stonewall and Lee, however, couldn't care less. They have become quite disenchanted with "the people," and though they still respond enough to earn their food, when alone they make cruel jokes at the expense of Ted and Sissy Rumpkin.

"Myron, what am I going to do?"

The Dangler has left its mark across Bambi's

abdomen and rib cage, the black dye of the rubber having apparently leached into her epidermis.

There was no alarm initially, but Bambi has returned from the kitchen sink with the following report: soap and water aren't even budging it.

What's the big deal, one might ask. Why should a few black streaks hinder a great inventor? Surely the marks will fade with time, probably be damn near invisible within a week or two.

Here's the problem:

Bambi may, indeed, be a great inventor, but as of yet, she is not a financially successful inventor. As of yet, she hasn't marketed a single one of her exercise inventions.

So, the black streaks will not hinder what she considers to be her "career and lifelong endeavor," but they will hinder her "day job," which is actually a night job at Heavenly Slice, a topless nightclub which Bambi prefers to call an "exotic dance theatre."

Bambi has noticed that some of the girls at Heavenly Slice dance with a glazed stare, looking right through the crisp-shirted businessmen, the muddy-booted laborers, and the giggle-faced school boys who are too occupied with breasts, legs, and the illusion of sex to notice that they are unnoticed. But not Bambi. She studies each of her clients with scientific curiosity. To her, the hours at Heavenly Slice are just one more experiment as she tests hypothesis after hypothesis, trying to understand how female flesh can short-wire the brains of half the population of the most enlightened species on earth.

Sensing that the mark on her abdomen may result in a temporary disruption of this experiment, Bambi asks anxiously, "Myron, what are we going to do?"

Myron goes out to his truck, a slightly rusting old Chevy heaped with toolboxes and hand tools for his tree house business. (Myron has inadvertently become one of the most successful tree house contractors in the Southeast; a space shuttle design he did for the son of a Richmond doctor several years ago caught the attention of several newspapers and magazines, and business hasn't slowed down since.) Myron retrieves from the glove compartment a plastic jar of Grub Out Industrial Strength Hand Cleaner.

Back inside, he kneels and rubs the cool gel over Bambi's skin, and she breathes a sigh of relief as the black marks vanish from her belly. She watches Myron's large, rough hands move gently over her body. She studies the balding area atop Myron's head, wondering what has set apart the few remaining strands of hair from those that have fled in great number. She thinks it appropriate for Myron to be balding. It seems fitting for her lover, her sage.

"Ow...Ow...Owwww!" Bambi exclaims, fanning her belly with flopping hands, moving to "Double Owwww" as the cleansing tingle of the industrial strength hand cleaner grows into a painful burning, and a large pink rash forms across her mid-section. Myron runs to the refrigerator, grabs a stick of butter, rushes back to Bambi, and circles the butter over her belly.

The pain subsides. But the rash remains.

"I'm so sorry," says Myron, looking up at her with sad eyes, grieved at having disappointed the one person in the world who makes him feel like a hero.

"It's all right," Bambi says. "I could use a few nights off, anyhow."

Bambi calls Marty Schwinn, the owner of Heavenly Slice, but is only halfway through the story of her rash when she hears a beep on the line. "Anyway, won't be in. Gotta go. Got another call." She is excited. It is her first chance to use call-waiting since she talked Myron into getting it added to their monthly phone service two weeks ago. She is disappointed when her first ever interrupter asks for Myron. "It's for you; I think it's your sister," she says, handing the phone to Myron, who scowls as he takes it from her.

"Yeah, who's this?...Sissy? I don't believe I know a Sissy," he says to the caller.

Sissy is the name the second Ted Rumpkin had

given to the second Mrs. Ted Rumpkin; and, virtually from his birth, the third Ted Rumpkin had fully accepted the responsibility of emulating the second Ted Rumpkin just as the second Ted Rumpkin had served as understudy to the first Ted Rumpkin who, when not counting the massive dollars created by his moonshine empire, had addressed his wife by the juvenile, yet somewhat endearing, label of "Sissy."

"Wait a second; I take that back," says Myron into the receiver. "I think my sister married a sissy." He gives a snort of self-amusement. "I'm just kidding, Tildy…You married an idiot, not a sissy."

Tildy, short for Matilda, Sissy Rumpkin's birth name. How, she wonders, can her brother not see the higher quality of even a silly name like Sissy, over the boulder-like sobriety of Matilda? It is, in her opinion, simply further evidence of her brother's complete lack of taste, the same lack of taste that enables him to live in a rundown shack with a prostitute named, of all things, "Bambi."

"Bambi's not a prostitute. She's an exotic artist… and an inventor. And, yes, that was her on the phone." Myron looks at Bambi. She is smiling over Myron's referring to her as an exotic artist. "No," says Myron to his sister, "I won't give her your love.

Besides, if you've finally found some, you should keep it."

Sissy Rumpkin hangs up the phone, finding it hard to believe she has just handed over her house for an entire week. She had asked Myron to keep the dogs at his house, but he argued that his yard wasn't fenced and that it wouldn't be right to keep the dogs cooped up inside for a week. "Besides, this way me and Bambi can look after the plants, too," he said, causing Sissy Rumpkin to fight back tears. Before Linda Coxdale's breasts, there had been a maid to look after the plants, but she became the first of the endless cutbacks.

Myron likes the idea of taking a week's vacation. The pirate ship tree house he's building for a proctologist's son in one of the tallest maples in Charlotte will just have to wait.

There remains one character in this story that we've yet to meet. Given the complexity of his background and

smoke and gravity

psychological makeup, we probably should have been introduced to Duke Stubbins before now, but we'll just have to pay attention for a while and see if we can make up for the late start.

At the moment, Duke is walking along a sidewalk in Midford, Ohio. It is a sunny day accented by a cold, early spring breeze. Duke wears a flannel shirt and jeans, his bald head covered in a ski cap to protect his ears from the chill of the wind.

Duke spends several hours every day walking along sidewalks of Midford. So far today he has taken four thousand nine hundred and seventy-two steps. Duke's brain keeps track of every step; at any moment he is aware of the number of paces he has taken during the day, the month, and the year.

His brain even keeps a running tally of the total number of steps he has taken since July 17, 1968, the day his two fathers died.

Duke is seven steps past five thousand for the day when he stops at Ernie's Hot Dog Stand. Ernie has been selling hot dogs on the sidewalk in Midford since July 19, 1968. Prior to July 17, he had been a chauffeur for Marve Stubbins, Duke's biological father.

"Howdy, Duke," says Ernie, throwing two wieners into buns and covering them with double relish and a splash of chili.

Duke raises his hand in greeting, like an Indian from an old western movie.

"Here you go. Two Duke specials."

Duke gives a nod of appreciation and heads off down the sidewalk, while Ernie makes two slashes on Duke's monthly tab.

Within three hundred and seventeen steps, Duke has finished his hot dogs and reached the Crossroads Tavern. He enters and takes a seat at the bar between two burly men dressed in green coveralls.

Molly Rendale, the jovial, heavyset barmaid, slides a draft beer to Duke and then heads to the kitchen with a tray of dirty mugs.

"Pretty day, ain't it?" says the man on his left.

Duke nods and takes a sip of his beer.

"My name's Roy," says the other man. "Me and Talvin just drove down from Minneapolis."

Duke turns and gives the man a nod. He reads the label on the man's coveralls: Randall's Nationwide Moving Service. Duke wonders if someone new is moving to Midford, or if the two are just passing through.

"Don't have much to say, do you?" asks Talvin.

Duke turns back to Talvin and shakes his head in agreement.

"Well, you'd be considered quite rude where I'm from. But maybe this just ain't a very friendly town," Talvin says, leaning close so that his breath forms a beery cloud around Duke's face.

Duke stands and walks over to the coat rack by the door (twelve steps), where he removes his ski cap and hangs it on a hook. Rather than returning to his stool, he finds a table in the corner (seventeen steps).

It is not long before the hulks in green coveralls slam their empty mugs on the bar and walk over to his table.

"Looks like we're out of beer and out of money," says Roy, looking down at Duke.

"Yep," says Talvin, "unless you're going to buy us another beer, looks like there ain't much left to do to kill time except fight."

Duke has never been in a fight in his life and figures the two Neanderthals in front of him wouldn't be a good place to start. As he rises to find Molly and buy two beers, a voice makes its way across the bar. The voice is made up of angry squeaks, like a mouse cussing a cat for eating its cheese.

"You want to mess with him, you're going to have to go through me first," pipe the short, rapidly fired sound waves.

The voice belongs to Decky Peteman, a jockey-sized man in his sixties, who is making his way across the bar.

Duke holds up his hands and tries to motion to Decky that everything's fine, that there's going to be no trouble, but Decky disagrees. He lunges head first, sinking his head into Talvin's excessive gut, his face disappearing into the green coveralls, causing Talvin to tumble to the floor as a thunderous belch erupts from the depths of his belly.

As Decky Peteman jumps to his feet, a broad smile stretches across his face. It has been years, decades even, since he has felt such a surge of victory.

As Roy cocks his fist to avenge his fallen partner, slumbering dendrites awaken in Duke's brain to receive a rush of adrenaline. Signals are sent to his arm that have never traveled through his nervous system before. In a flash Duke's hand has balled itself into a fist and landed upon Roy's jaw, sending him sprawling over Talvin.

If time could be stopped at this instant, Decky and Duke could live out their lives as proud and victorious warriors, but alas, this story is being told in a linear universe where time must move on. However, before it does, let's take a look backwards and give the two a chance to enjoy their temporary triumph.

Duke grew up with two fathers: his biological father, Marve Stubbins; and his biological father's lover, Harold Brimwall. Marve Stubbins was a loving man, but very quiet, very serious. Marve Stubbins was the founder of Stubbins Jams and Jellies, which to this day remains the largest employer in Midford. Without the jobs and money flowing through the jam factory, it is likely that Midford would evaporate within a few years.

Marve Stubbins fell in love with Harold Brimwall because Harold was neither quiet, nor serious. Around town, in their crisp gray suits and their well-groomed heads of thick, dark hair with scatterings of stately silver, the two were nearly indistinguishable.

But once back at their secluded house several miles outside the Midford city limits, the two could not be more different. For Marve Stubbins, the tie remained as he went to his study to ponder business matters, but we should note his late hours were not for his own benefit. By the time he was thirty-five, Marve Stubbins had made all the money his simple desires would ever demand, but Marve Stubbins felt a tremendous obligation to all of the employees at Stubbins Jams and Jellies. He thought of himself as the Mother of Midford. And while he always made sure to leave time for young Duke, it was Harold who spent countless hours of play and mischief with the boy. Duke referred to his biological father as Pappa and to his play partner as Daddy.

Duke's favorite pastime as a boy was a game he and Harold called Catch the Fairy. Harold, wearing a cotton skirt or silk kimono, would hide in the woods which he and Duke had filled with rope swings and ladders leading to wooden platforms high in the trees. Duke would swing through the air, chasing Harold from platform to platform. At the end of the game, when the boy had captured the fairy, the two of them would go to the largest tree in the woods, and thank the Oak Goddess for guiding them through the trees.

"Dear Goddess," the young Duke would pray, "thank you for giving Daddy and me the gift of flight and letting us return gently to your earth. And please be with Pappa as he looks after the people of Midford."

Also living in the house with Duke and his two fathers was Novella Lee, the housekeeper. Novella Lee was the only black person young Duke had ever known, and her dark, fleshy body was an object of abundant wonder for him.

Novella Lee was also the administrator of the household. She cleaned and cooked meals, ordered the groceries, paid the bills, decided when carpet needed replacing, and with Harold's assistance, planned the elaborate parties that were held every few months for the jam workers and their families, which meant most of Midford. The workers seemed to favor costume parties, so at least four times a year the house was filled with ex-presidents, devils, famous ball players, Marie Antoinette, Napoleon, and at least one person impersonating Marve Stubbins.

Novella Lee always came up with enough categories

to make sure that everyone left with a prize for his or her costume. Most Original. Most Indecipherable. Longest Dead, etc. The grand prize for best costume almost always went to a jar topper at the factory, who spent most of his time away from the factory preparing his costume for the next party. That jar topper was Decky Peteman.

"Let's move this party outside," Harold had proclaimed during what would be the last masquerade extravaganza before the crash that would claim the lives of Duke's Pappa and Daddy.

The woods were soon filled with exhilarated cries as history's most famous characters flew through the trees on the rope swings.

Decky Peteman had come dressed as the Spirit of St. Louis, with large balsa wings springing from his trunk. After filling his small body with champagne, and after several successful swings from platform to platform, Decky eventually slipped and went plummeting to the ground.

Duke watched with horror as Decky's playful roar turned to a terrified shriek.

Even before Decky hit the ground, Duke was running for the house to get Novella Lee who just happened to be dressed as Florence Nightingale for the evening.

Novella Lee and Duke reached the crash site to find Decky in a tangle of balsa and cardboard, laughing nervously. He was quite shaken, but uninjured, the balsa wings having slowed his descent just enough to prevent catastrophe.

Duke said a prayer of thanks to the Oak Goddess and the party returned inside

Decky Peteman may have survived his fall, but he never forgave himself when two weeks later Marve Stubbins' twin-engine plane went down for no apparent reason as Marve and Harold were returning from a jelly convention in upstate New York, killing Marve instantly while Harold would live for several more hours before dying in the county hospital. Decky was convinced that in some horrible, mystical way his crash the night of the masquerade party had brought about the tragedy.

The day of the crash, Duke skipped home from his school bus singing a song he and Harold had invented the night before Harold and Marve left for the convention. "My tummy may get empty, the river may rise high, but nothing bothers me, because I can fly. I can fly. I can fly."

When he reached the drive, Duke sprinted for the house, expecting to find his fathers returned from their trip, but all he found instead was a somber Novella

Lee, who had spent the day crying, in hopes of not crying in front of the boy.

"Your Pappa's dead," she said, reaching to surround Duke with her large, fat-pillowed arms.

The boy's body collapsed, and he sobbed into her arms while she explained about the crash.

"Where's Daddy?" Duke asked.

"He's in the hospital."

"Is he going to live?"

Novella Lee squeezed Duke tightly and told him the truth. "I don't know."

The hospital was more than three miles away, and though Novella Lee could have called the factory to have Ernie come with the car, she chose to walk, thinking that Duke could use the time to be with his thoughts.

During the walk, Duke tried to imagine what death would be like. Harold had said once that death was no big deal, but that it was something different for everybody. He'd said it was like the final performance of a long-running play. After months together, the cast would move on to something else, each with a foggy image of what lay in store for their individual journeys, and this destiny each would approach with a mix of apprehension and expectation.

Harold lay swollen on his bed, his body fully painted with bruised color, his face unrecognizable.

Duke took Harold's mangled hand in his own. "You're going to die, aren't you, Daddy?"

"Yes, I'm afraid that's the way I'd have to bet," Harold said, forming a smile with his mouthful of broken teeth.

Over the next several hours, Harold passed to and from consciousness, his mind afloat with opiates the nurses administered every thirty minutes.

Novella Lee found a comfortable chair outside Harold's room and went to sleep while Duke remained bedside, more alert than he'd ever been in his life. If his Daddy were headed to another performance, he hoped to get a glimpse of where the next theatre might be found.

It was just before midnight when Harold made his last break into conscious awareness. As his eyes met Duke's, a sense of urgency charged through the opiates that clouded his thoughts.

"Duke," he said, struggling for voice.

"Yes, Daddy?"

"I'll be flying," and with that, Harold left the stage.

Duke and Novella Lee made the walk home in silence, Novella Lee prepared to give the boy whatever she could, but not wanting to encroach on the boy's sorrow and reflection.

Duke felt as if he should feel deep pain, felt as though he should know something now that he hadn't known before. But as far as he could tell, he had not changed. He knew that the future held countless moments in which he would yearn for the company of his fathers. He knew he would never catch another fairy. He knew he would never look up and see the light in his Pappa's window and know that Midford was being looked after. So, yes, things had changed, but it seemed to Duke that he should have gained something to counter the losses. There was nothing. Loss replaced by nothing. His thoughts bounced around his mind, seeking the gift of experience that would transform the death of his fathers into some useful piece in the puzzle of his life, some quick gush of agony that would leave behind a magical rose. But still nothing.

As Novella Lee and Duke reached the house, Duke searched for a place that would bring tears to his eyes, for he wanted desperately to cry, but when he looked into his mind all he found was this: It had taken exactly five thousand steps to walk silently home from the hospital.

Myron and Bambi rumble into Timber Haven on Myron's old Yamaha motorcycle. The motorcycle is one of Myron's six great passions, the other five being his backyard, Bambi, boomerangs, bourbon, and tomato sandwiches.

Myron and Bambi are wearing matching outfits of cut-off jeans and white t-shirts. Myron wears his workboots, while Bambi is barefooted, and on her back Bambi has a knapsack containing their toothbrushes, three boomerangs, and the Dangler prototype with two strands of undyed rubber.

They pull into the Rumpkin driveway and dismount. The garage door is open, and Myron, unaware of the severity of the Rumpkin's financial losses, is puzzled to find it occupied by two mid-range Japanese sedans.

Inside, Sissy Rumpkin gives her brother a rigid hug and Bambi a leaden handshake before leading them upstairs where she goes over a short list of instructions. "The dogs are to be fed once a day, two scoops each, and just water the plants enough to dampen the soil."

"Got that, Bambi?" says Myron, "water the dogs twice a day, but just enough to dampen them."

Sissy Rumpkin doesn't laugh. "And please don't bother bringing in the newspaper or the mail." Sissy wants to be sure the neighbors know she and Ted are vacationing.

As they walk down the hall towards the guest bedroom, Myron opens the door to the master bedroom in which rests a pond-sized hot tub at the foot of a large canopy bed. Sissy pretends not to notice, but Myron enters the master bedroom and calls down the hall, "Tildy, or Sissy, or whoever you are, me and Bambi should probably stay in this room. Bambi's been having allergy problems and some time in the hot tub might just open her sinuses right up."122%

Bambi's face curls into a questioning look, and she is about to ask what allergy problems, when Myron winks at her with a broad grin. "Ain't that right, Sweetie?"

You've probably noticed that there is much tension, maybe even a degree of dislike, between Myron and his sister, but what is the origin of this sibling conflict? For a better understanding, let's take a look from the very beginning. Better yet, let's take a look from well before the very beginning:

In January of 1953, a truck driver by the name of Frank Fugate was driving a truckload of cigarettes from Virginia to Florida. Frank was thirty-four and loved his job. His father had never been able to afford a car and died without ever driving an automobile. This made Frank especially appreciative of the opportunity to drive every day and to be paid for doing so. His only plan in life was to drive a truck until he died.

It was evening on this particular day in January of 1953, and as Frank eyed a peeling billboard for Harriet's Hungry House, he realized he was quite hungry. Along the bottom of the billboard Frank read the words "Truckers Welcomed," and these words were the decisive factor that led his strong forearms to turn the wheel and send his rig into the gravel parking lot.

He found himself to be the only customer in Harriet's Hungry House and took a seat in one of the booths along the wall. However, he was soon reprimanded when a lone waitress appeared.

"Can't you read, Mister," said the waitress, pointing to a sign on the wall:

BOOTHS RESERVED FOR
PARTIES OF THREE OR MORE

"But I'm the only one in here," argued Frank, stating the obvious.

"A rule's a rule," said the woman as she walked

behind the counter and waited for Frank to vacate the booth, which he did after exhaling a breath of disbelief.

"What will it be?" the waitress asked as he took a seat on one of the stools.

The woman was fairly young, her body incorporating feminine curves around a sturdy frame. Frank found her attractive, but as he studied her, the one thing that stood out to him was her eyes. The young woman had ancient eyes, full of conflict and despair, eyes that shrank into a mean-spirited squint as she repeated her question, "What will it be?...Or did you mistake this place for a hotel?"

"What's the day's special?" Frank asked.

"Meatloaf and cabbage."

"I'll take it," Frank said.

"Too bad. We're out... How about a grilled cheese and grits," the woman said, flipping her pad shut and tossing two slices of bread on the griddle before Frank had a chance to respond.

"Sure, sounds great," Frank said in hopes of avoiding total defeat. The waitress gave him another threatening squint as she grabbed a cigarette from her purse and took a seat at the booth from which Frank had been recently evicted.

As the woman took the last puffs of her cigarette, the smoke rising from Frank's grilled cheese grew thicker. By the time the sandwich made its way to Frank's plate, the sandwich was charred on one side, uncooked on the other, and floating on a bed of cold grits.

Frank promptly wolfed down the sandwich, ate every grain of the cold grits, paid his tab, and left a shiny penny beside his plate as a tip. Frank tried to slam the door on his way out, but the pressurized closer brought it to a gentle, shushing close.

At this point, it looked certain that Frank Fugate would resume his trip to Florida, taking with him his DNA, half of which would be needed for the waitress to produce two of the main characters of this story.

But as fate would have it, the genetic struggle for replication was given another chance when Frank turned the key and his rig responded with silence.

Frank worked for almost an hour under the hood in the dark and cold before capitulating and going back into the diner to drink a cup of coffee and think things over.

"Back so soon, big tipper?" the waitress mocked him.

Frank acted surprised. "Oh my God, I forgot to tip you, didn't I? Well, here," he said, slapping a pair of quarters on the counter. "By the way, have you seen my lucky penny?"

The waitress slid a plastic wastebasket towards Frank. "I think you'll find it in there," she told him.

"Oh, it was just a silly superstition, anyway," replied Frank, sliding the wastebasket back towards the waitress. "I was wondering if I could get a cup of coffee."

"Don't see why not, but you'll have to wait for it to brew."

"Guess, I've got the time," Frank said, taking a seat on a stool. "Look, I've been on the road all day. Would you mind terribly if I stretched out my legs in one of the booths?"

The woman felt bad. She had no reason to have been so rude to the man. He wasn't the source of her gloom and fury.

Earlier that day she had received a letter from her boyfriend of seven years, Les Minor, who had left three months earlier for the Texas oil fields where the jobs were plentiful and the pay good. The plan was for Les to work six months, save up some money, and then come back to North Carolina so the two of them could get married.

The letter had been to inform her there had been a change in plans. Les wasn't coming back.

We should note that the waitress's rudeness had not kept Frank from being attracted to her, for Frank's DNA was, of course, of the male variety, always prepared to cast its seeds into any available field, and the waitress was much more than any old field, for she had a small waist and plump hips, creating a waist-to-hip ratio that Frank's DNA knew to be ideal, a place where one might be replicated quite nicely.

"I'm sorry if I've been rude," the woman said, motioning for Frank to sit in the booth.

She then started the coffee brewing, took a seat opposite him, lit a cigarette, and launched into the history and details of her ill-fated romance with Les.

"This Les must be a very stupid man," Frank said, causing the woman to smile. "My name's Frank, by the way."

The woman's smile broadened. "Mine's Francie," she said.

This was a fortunate break for our story because, for reasons unknown, a statistically disproportionate number of couples have alliterative first names. However, at this point there still was nothing within Francie's hips that was even entertaining the idea of sharing DNA with Frank. She needed more than a quick wit and a handsome face. Her well-suited hips needed someone who'd stay around for awhile, stay around for a couple of decades at least, and a man who made his living by keeping on the move did not seem like a likely candidate. Still, it was nice to have someone to share her misery with.

"What's it like being on the road all the time?" she asked Frank.

"I guess it's something you either love or hate. I love it. I like seeing things. Mountains. Cities. Trees.

Factories. Deer. Bums. It's all beautiful to me."

"Even rude waitresses?"

"Especially rude waitresses," Frank assured her, causing Francie's eyes to lose a bit of their heaviness and twinkle with a youthfulness more appropriate for her years.

"What's wrong with your truck?"

"Don't know. Can't figure it out."

Frank's rig had never failed him before. He was a fanatic about maintenance, and was capable of completely disassembling an engine and putting it back together with little more than a pair of pliers and a pocketknife.

The only explanation was that fate had crawled under the hood.

"How far to the nearest hotel?" he asked Francie.

"Nothing between here and Charlotte."

"How far out am I?"

"About thirty miles."

"You're kidding!"

"Nope…"

"Damn. Looks like I'll be sleeping in the rig."

Francie took a drag of her cigarette and thought over the situation.

"Look, it would be good for me to have company tonight. You can sleep on my couch."

It was an innocent proposal, an injured woman comforting herself by helping out a stranger in need.

He would spend the night on her couch, they would wake in the morning and shake hands, and then he would disappear down the road, never to be thought of again.

That's how it was supposed to go, and that's the way it would have gone had it not been for a simple misunderstanding.

Francie lived in an attic apartment above her great-aunt's house, and Francie made Frank remove his shoes before they navigated the flight of rickety wooden steps that led to her apartment.

"I thought you said your aunt was deaf," Frank said.

"I said almost deaf... and very prudish. She'd have a stroke if she even thought I had a man upstairs."

Frank ascended the steps slowly, gently placing one foot before lifting the other, taking over three minutes to make the summit and enter Francie's apartment where he found Francie holding a spewing bottle of champagne over the sink.

"I was saving this for me and Les when he came back," she said, handing Frank a glass of champagne.

"No need letting it turn to pickle juice," Frank said, taking the glass, which was actually a washed out jelly jar. "Nice place you've got here."

And it was nice, in a very simple, warm way. The furnishings in the living area consisted of a yellow rocking chair with a cane seat, an old brown sofa with a crocheted afghan draped over the back, a phonograph, and a small bookcase with a bible and several leather-bound books.

Frank sat in the rocker and Francie on the couch.

"Here's to strangers, and to hell with Texas oil fields," said Frank, raising his glass. Francie smiled and the two drank to the toast.

Neither Frank nor Francie was in the habit of consuming alcohol. Frank had spent a few beer-laden years in his late teens, but had not seen much of the bottle since he first started driving trucks for a living. Francie's purchase of the celebratory champagne represented her first alcohol purchase ever. It did not take long for Frank and Francie to feel the bubbles flowing through their brains.

By the time the champagne bottle found itself sitting empty on the kitchen counter, Francie's' flesh was standing before her DNA board asking for an overnight pass. The board firmly denied this request.

Francie's debate with the board caused a lull in conversation. During this lull, Frank was having his own argument. His DNA board was demanding that he act. Grab her. Kiss her. Just see what happens. It's worth a shot.

Frank sternly disobeyed these commands. The woman had been very generous, and Frank did not want to repay generosity on her part with asininity on his.

"Maybe we should get some sleep," he said.

"Yes, that's probably a good idea," she agreed.

His board of DNA sank in defeat. Hers sighed with relief.

Francie prepared the couch, draping it with a frayed cotton sheet.

After Frank washed up and brushed his teeth, he lay down on the couch and Francie covered him with a quilt her grandmother had made decades earlier, small snowflakes dancing around a snowflake queen. She then went to her bedroom, returned with her favorite pillow, and tucked it gently under Frank's head.

As she smiled and bid him goodnight, it suddenly occurred to Francie's bubbly mind that she had dominated the night's conversation with stories of herself and that she knew nothing of the stranger who would be leaving in the morning.

"By the way, Frank, where's home?"

Francie wanted to know where he had spent his childhood. Had he grown up in one place, or had his family moved around, preparing Frank for a life on the road? She might have asked, "Where were you born?" or "Where did you grow up?" or simply said,

"Tell me about your childhood." Instead she had chosen, "Where's home?"

"Right here," Frank said as a wave of appreciation rolled across his face.

What Frank meant was that he was always home, whether in a park, a truckstop, or a barbershop. Because he had no home, Frank was always home. But Francie's bubbly mind interpreted his response to mean that after years of not knowing where he belonged, he had finally found home.

For the first time all night, Francie's DNA board considered her request for an overnight pass, and Francie's flesh seized the opportunity.

At first, Frank took it to be a simple goodnight kiss, but it was soon obvious that it was much more. Within the hour Matilda (Sissy) Fugate (Rumpkin) was conceived, exactly one half of her being genetically Frank, and one half Francie.

The following morning Frank and Francie woke simultaneously and wiggled free from their entanglement on the couch. After a breakfast of grilled cheese sandwiches and grits, they made their way downstairs where they were spotted by Francie's great-aunt who was walking up the drive with the newspaper.

"Francie! What do you think..."

"Don't worry, ma'am. I've taken care of everything," Frank chimed in. "You shouldn't be seeing any more of those roaches." If her sight had been better, Francie's great-aunt could have easily recognized Frank to be a contented man who was coming from a night of love and not a conscientious pest controller who had made an early morning emergency visit to a client in despair.

"What roaches?"

"I didn't want to alarm you, Auntie. I've been seeing roaches around lately, but Frank says we shouldn't have any more problems."

"Well, thank you, dear," she said, giving Frank's face a pat and heading inside where she took a seat by the window and enjoyed the energy she had received by her brush with two youngsters in love.

Francie drove Frank to his truck. The fate vapors had evaporated from his engine and the truck revved up effortlessly, sending a wave of excitement and sadness through the couple.

No questions were asked. No promises made.

"Thanks for a wonderful night," Frank said as he put the truck in gear and disappeared down the road.

For four years, Frank would relive that January night as he rolled down the highway. You might think the experience would lead Frank to search out other encounters, but this was not the case. Great truckers have one thing in common: a stellar imagination, an imagination that cannot only dream up new adventures, but also relive old ones with an acuity that surpasses even the original event.

For four years, Frank danced with Francie on that old couch. For four years, he stayed drunk on that bottle of cheap champagne and kept his belly full with those grilled cheese sandwiches and grits.

In January of 1957, Frank was on a Maryland interstate headed for New Jersey, hauling a truckload of processed chicken parts. As the gizzards and livers sloshed about in their jars of chicken juice, and Frank day-dreamt of holding Francie's skin against his, a chill ran through his body, followed by a dizziness that sent the cab spinning like a carousel.

Initially, he thought it was merely a silly schoolboy reaction to his thoughts of Francie, but soon the tingling grew to explosive pain.

Frank lost consciousness, and when he awoke he was surrounded by the sterile light of a Baltimore hospital room, his body in a suit of plaster armor.

"You've had a heart attack," a young, pimply-faced doctor said to him.

"A heart attack? I'm too young to have a heart attack," Frank argued.

"Unfortunately not," countered the doctor. "It was a major attack. Apparently, you became unconscious and your truck took out several trees. You're very lucky to be alive."

"Aren't we all?" Frank grinned nervously.

"Are there any family members you'd like for us to call?" the doctor asked.

The grin disappeared from Frank's face. "No, there's no one," he said softly.

The Frank Fugate family was something that had always been real to him, but it had always existed in the future. He considered himself a young man, and assumed one day he'd wake up and feel like a father and be surrounded by a wife and kids.

As he lay in his plaster suit with a bad heart and more bones broken than not, he realized he had, indeed, awakened to find himself no longer young, but there was no family in sight.

He remained in the hospital for seven weeks. For the first few weeks, the body cast made reading impossible, and though there was a radio in his room, his roommate, a retired school principal, seemed always to be asleep whenever Frank was in the mood for some music. So out of politeness and self-pity, Frank spent most of his time in the hospital staring blankly at the wall, dreaming of Francie, dreaming the two of them had stayed together, looking after her

Auntie and raising a flock of young Fugates.

Therefore, it was not surprising that upon his release from the hospital, his body cast having shrunk to a full cast on his left leg, he hobbled into the bus station and purchased a ticket for North Carolina, his intent not to start a family, but merely to thank Francie for providing him with the pleasant thoughts that helped to pass the time during his hospital stay. From North Carolina, he planned to continue south, to the Keys maybe, to live in a tent and fish until he had recuperated enough to go back on the road.

As the bus approached Harriet's Hungry House, Frank read a small roadside sign:
WELCOME TO PICKETT

est. October 17, 1953

"Right here," he said, tapping the bus driver on the shoulder. The bus rolled into the Harriet's Hungry House parking lot and came to a stop in almost the exact spot Frank's truck had occupied a few years earlier. Frank hobbled down the steps and retrieved his large canvas duffel bag from the cargo bay.

As the bus pulled away, Frank stood in the parking lot not knowing what to expect. As he thought things through, he began to feel ridiculous. What if Francie didn't even remember him? Or, even worse, what if she pitied him for hanging on to something she had long ago forgotten? Frank had nine hundred dollars in his pocket, disability compensation from Drexel Trucking, and he considered spending some of it on a cab ride to Charlotte.

After much debate, he decided to at least go in for a bite to eat. There'd be no shame in that. If Francie recognized him, he'd think for a moment and then pretend to pluck her name from the back of his mind.

It was lunchtime, and the diner was full. Frank found a vacant seat at the counter and took a seat as best he could with the leg cast clunking against the neighboring stool.

"What'll it be?" a large, wrinkled woman demanded.

"What's the special?" Frank asked, surveying the room for Francie.

"BLT and fries," answered the waitress.

"I'll take it."

Other than the large, pruny woman who had taken his order, Frank counted three other employees: two scrawny waitresses who could be anorexic twins, and a cook with slicked back hair and a peach fuzz mustache.

A mixed wave of disappointment and relief swept over Frank as he realized Francie was not around. He envisioned her in Charlotte, married to a doctor or lawyer or banker, someone with scads of money who'd stopped in for a meal on his way home from a hunting trip.

Or maybe things had not gone so well for her. Perhaps she'd searched for months to find him after their night together, and in the end had lost hope and taken her own life rather than spending a lifetime of aching for her true love.

Or maybe it was her day off.

The large waitress brought his BLT, and as casually as he could he asked, "Is Francie coming in today?"

The waitress cocked her head. "Francie hasn't worked here in over two years. Why do you ask?"

Frank took a sip of coffee. "I'm just an old friend," he said.

The waitress crossed her arms and studied Frank as he took a bite of his sandwich. "Your name wouldn't be Frank, would it?"

Frank swallowed. "As a matter of fact, it would be."

The large woman began jumping up and down, sending waves of rippling flesh rolling over her body. "It's Frank!" she exclaimed to the rest of the diner. "It's Frank!"

Dozens of overall-clad farmers and workers stared at Frank and the waitress in confusion.

"What in the hell are you going on about?" asked one of the bony waitresses.

"It's Frank! It's Francie's Frank!"

The bony waitress approached and studied Frank. "Francie's Frank? Are you sure?"

The large woman was panting and trying to catch her breath. "Go ahead. Ask him yourself," she said between breaths.

"Well, is you or ain't you?" she asked, staring sternly into Frank's eyes.

Frank was bewildered. He didn't know how to answer. Was it possible that he was, indeed, "Francie's Frank"?

"You come through here about four years ago driving a rig?" pressed the bony waitress.

Frank nodded. "Yes...It broke down and Francie helped me out."

"I'd say she did a little better than just help out." A smile spread across the waitress's face. "It's him," she declared.

The restaurant erupted in cheers and applause. Before he knew what was happening, a trio of farmers plucked Frank from his stool, carried him outside, and placed Frank and his bag in the bed of their truck where he found himself surrounded by rusted hand tools, muddy boots, and empty beer cans.

The diner emptied, and the patrons loaded in their vehicles and followed the old pick-up, forming a parade that ended at Francie's great-aunt's house.

The farmers helped Frank out of the truck and motioned him towards the house. Not knowing what else to do, Frank knocked on the door to announce his arrival to Francie's Auntie.

A little girl opened the door, reaching above her head to hold the knob.

"Who is it, Tildy?" a voice called. Frank

recognized it as Francie's voice, and his uncasted leg grew weak.

"It's a man with a plastic leg," said the girl.

"It's Frank," he called in a shaky voice. "You helped me a few years ago when…"

His words were cut off as Francie charged him with a hug. "Oh, Frank. I knew you'd come back. I knew it."

Frank could make no sense of the situation. How could he have been expected to? He had no way of knowing that exactly nine months after his overnight stay, on the very day that Pickett was staging a festival to commemorate its birth as a town, Francie had given birth to a healthy baby girl.

How was he to know that two hours after the birth of his daughter, Francie's Auntie had passed away?

And how could he have known that the town had hired a gypsy fortune teller for the festival who had proclaimed that the father of the baby had been sent by the spirits to father the child who would offset the loss of Francie's Auntie?

And how could he have known that two hundred drunk farmers at a festival would keep alive the legend of the spirit father and declare it Pickett's official legend?

"I knew it. I just knew it," Francie continued, her arms tight around Frank's neck.

53

That evening, after Francie had tucked Tildy into her bed, Francie and Frank tiptoed up to Francie's old apartment, where they threw a blanket over the dusty couch and began what would be a week of torrid lovemaking.

At some point during the week, Frank's DNA once again merged with Francie's. Nine months later Myron Fugate was born.

For young Tildy, the months leading up to Myron's birth were full of happiness.

Frank and Francie married in the summer and the Fugates became the unofficial first family of Pickett. Between Francie's inheritance and Frank's disability pay, the couple had enough money not to work for a while and spent most of their hours enjoying and entertaining Tildy.

It was difficult for Frank to believe that Tildy had been toddling around the earth for over three years without his knowledge. He had been larger than he knew, and even if he hadn't survived his heart attack, his genes would have danced on.

Frank, Francie, and Tildy took most of their lunches at Hibbs Park. They'd stop by Harriet's Hungry House and pick up a few sandwiches and fries and then head out to the park for a picnic, their picnic blanket being the very quilt upon which Tildy had been conceived.

Tildy's favorite after-lunch activity was "silly sledding," for which Frank would tie a rope to a large trash can lid, tie the other end around his waist, and then place little Tildy on the lid and tug her around the high grass outfield of the baseball diamond.

In the early days of silly sledding, Francie would follow behind Tildy and her stallion father with the camera to capture the adventure on film, but as her pregnancy progressed, Francie took more and more to after-lunch naps, the sun warming her face as she gently circled her palms over the growing life inside her.

Frank's excitement and anticipation grew exponentially with Francie's belly. Tildy was the biggest happiness he'd ever known, and the thought of yet another child, another bundle of electric joy, was as much as Frank could ask of life.

On the evening of December 17, 1957, Frank was in the kitchen cleaning up after a dinner of spaghetti and meatballs when Francie called from the living room. Frank sprang into action.

The hospital was exactly thirty-five minutes away. Frank had timed it on three different practice runs, allowing three minutes to drop Tildy off at Harriet's Hungry House to be looked after by the lucky wait staff on duty which turned out to be Priscilla, the large woman who had first recognized Frank as "Francie's

Frank," and Angelica, one of the anorexic twins.

As Frank and Francie rolled into the hospital parking lot, it occurred to Frank that Francie had done all this before. For a moment or two, a sadness drifted through him, a regret for having missed the beginning of Tildy's life, but the regret quickly washed away when Francie's water broke as they entered the broad doors of the hospital.

At the entrance of the maternity ward, Frank was directed to a large waiting room with a coffee table covered in magazines and walls lined with folding chairs and an old sofa.

Two other expectant fathers had taken up their posts in the waiting room. On the far wall, a neatly groomed man in a navy suit sat smoking a cigarette as if it were a straw and he were sucking the remnants of a milkshake from the bottom of a large paper cup, while the man on the near wall leaned back into his chair, casually skimming through the newspaper.

Frank took a seat for a moment, then stood and paced a lap around the room while the other two men watched bemusedly. After a second lap, Frank forced himself to sit again.

The magazines on the coffee table were several months old. Frank studied the collection and contemplated the events of the year which would soon culminate with the birth of his second child.

It had been a year mixed with conflict and

achievement. The United States was struggling internally with racial relations and true equality while engaging in an external battle with the Soviets in the race to conquer space. Neither challenge was going particularly well. President Eisenhower had been forced to deploy a thousand paratroopers in Arkansas to assure the admittance of nine black students into the halls of Little Rock Central High. In the space race, the Soviets had launched Sputnik!I into orbit. Frank always searched the evening sky, hoping not to find it. It made him feel the same way as finding trash on an empty beach. The U.S., on the other hand, had only managed to pollute the virgin space with two small aluminum pellets.

Frank browsed the magazines for more hopeful signs.

In November, Michigan had connected its upper and lower peninsulas with the world's largest suspension bridge. Frank smiled as he read about the multi-million dollar project.

"Our children will be born in the year of bridges," he heard himself say to the man in the navy suit.

The proclamation took the man by surprise, and not knowing how to respond, he held his cigarette case open to Frank. "Care for a smoke?" he asked.

Despite the fact that he did not smoke, and despite the fact that he had just read in one of the coffee table magazines that the surgeon general had reviewed studies that seemed to indicate a possible link between smoking and lung cancer, Frank took a cigarette from the silver case.

"First time?" the man asked.

"Smoking?"

"No. Kids," said the man. "It's my fourth, and if this one isn't a girl, I'm not taking it home."

"It's my second," said Frank, the regret of missing Tildy's birth lessened by his realization that his role was to be played out predominantly in the waiting room among strangers.

"You know what scares me most about bringing a kid into this world today?" the man asked.

"What's that?"

"The Dodgers... Just up and moving like that. Where is this world heading?"

The Brooklyn Dodgers had moved to the West Coast. Frank's only thought on the matter involved the physical act of moving. How many truckloads did it take to move a baseball team? How many bats would be making the transcontinental journey? Gloves? Desks? Uniforms? In all his trucking days, he had never hauled any part of a sports team.

"A person needs things he can count on," the man said. It was obvious that for him the Brooklyn Dodgers had been one of those things.

What Frank was thinking was this: maybe one of the fundamental traits of being human is the need to worry about something. He had just read a tableful of atomic bombs and espionage. Disease and murder. Mobsters and random hatred. But out of all the possibilities, this man had chosen the infidelity of a sports team on which to rest his despair.

After only thirty minutes and two more of the suited man's cigarettes, a nurse walked into the waiting room and announced, "Congratulations, Mr. Fugate. You have a beautiful, healthy son."

Frank was confused. It wasn't his turn yet; he felt as if he were breaking in line at the deli.

"I'm sorry. There must be some mistake," he was uttering, but his objection was drowned out by slaps on the back and congratulatory exclamations from the other two men.

The nurse led Frank to the recovery room where Francie lay drugged and shrouded.

"I love you," she mumbled.

"And I love you," Frank said, and as he bent over his wife and held her, he felt the love in his blood. At that moment it made sense to him that the heart had been elected the organ of devotion. It was more than a symbol; it was truth. Blood as truth.

"Have you seen him?" Francie asked.

"Not yet."

"He's beautiful."

"I know," Frank said, kissing his wife on the forehead.

As Frank walked down the glaring white hall to the nursery he knew with a fundamental, vivid certainty that things were exactly as they should be.

For half an hour Frank stood outside the window of the nursery, entranced with his son. Behind the new little person, a young nurse smiled and directed exaggerated facial expressions to the other babies. But as Frank looked at his son, it was not joyful silliness, but rather a solemn sense of awe which consumed him.

When he was in high school a biology teacher had told his class about African gazelles and how it was not uncommon for a newborn to spring from his mother as she galloped along with the herd fleeing a hungry lion, and how the newborn gazelle literally hit the ground running, keeping pace with the rest of the herd. The idea had fascinated Frank. What was going on inside the head of the infant gazelle? Did it want to stop and ask a few questions? Where are we going? What's the hurry?

Or did the youngster already know? The teacher had suggested the possibility of an ancient gazelle wisdom that was passed on as surely as the four legs and elegant horns. As Frank watched his son lie peacefully in his crib, he found it easy to believe the teacher's theory, easy to believe there were many things, deep and mysterious things, that his tiny son already knew.

A nurse brought a pink baby girl into the nursery and placed her two cribs away from Frank's son. Even through the glass he could hear the shrill song which burst from her lungs.

Within minutes, the man in the blue suit appeared, wearing a broad smile.

"Look at my little angel," he said as the nurse held her up for inspection.

"She's beautiful," Frank offered.

The man produced two cigars from his coat pocket and held one out for Frank. "My name's Stan, by the way. Stan Noffsinger."

"Frank Fugate," Frank said, accepting the cigar.

For the duration of the cigars, Frank and Stan exchanged clichés.

"The future of the world is lying in those cribs," Frank said.

To which Stan responded, "Not that they know it. Look at them. Not a care in the world."

A few minutes later a nurse pulled the nursery curtains closed. "It's bedtime, gentlemen. You can come back in the morning."

As Frank reluctantly began to turn away, his small son reached for him, as if begging him to stay.

"I'll be back," Frank promised.

Frank realized that though he had asked countless questions about getting to the hospital, about the treatment of Francie, about making arrangements for

61

Tildy, he had not spent a single moment considering what he would do with himself after the birth.

He found a phone and called to check on Tildy.

"She's sound asleep," Priscilla informed him. "Why don't you just wait and come by in the morning?" Priscilla was excited to learn that the baby was a seven-pound baby boy, meaning she would win the Hungry House weight and gender pool.

"What's his name?" she asked. At the baby shower, she had suggested Myron as a boy's name.

"We haven't decided yet," Frank said, "but Myron's still a possibility."

From the dimly lit parking lot, Frank studied the windows of the hospital, some of which were still brightly lit, forming a constellation of sorts. He sent Francie a silent kiss, and was getting in his car when someone called his name from across the parking lot. It was Stan Noffsinger.

"I think we deserve a drink, Frankie Boy."

"Sounds fun, but I better be getting home."

"Come on. Just a quick one. I know a great little watering hole just down the street."

"Okay. I guess I have time for one," Frank capitulated.

He followed Stan less than a mile to the dirt parking lot of the Lucky Harpoon Tavern. The entrance to the Lucky Harpoon was guarded by two ceramic mermaids with watermelon-size breasts. Harpoons extended from their clutched hands and intersected above the doorway.

The mermaids were the fanciest thing about the Lucky Harpoon, the inside consisting of a plywood bar, cinderblock walls, and a dozen patrons scattered around metal tables and chairs.

The mood of the place immediately lifted when Stan pounded his fist on the bar. "A shot of whiskey for everyone, please, Mr. Barkeep."

The bartender, a large blonde man who Frank assumed to be the owner of the tavern, lined up a row of shot glasses and filled them one by one as the assembled men and women gathered at the bar.

Once everyone had picked up their free booze, Stan raised his glass into the air. "Here's to the two youngest, most beautiful people in the world, and here's to their lucky fathers and beautiful mothers."

Glasses clinked and whiskey disappeared.

The liquor burned in Frank's throat as the strangers immersed him in hugs and slaps.

"Barkeep, another round," Stan called over the ruckus.

A woman in a tight lavender sweater and matching skirt walked behind the bar and placed a stack of records on an old phonograph. As the bartender lined up another round, polka music bounced from the walls.

Frank took his second shot in several quick sips

before the woman who had played the polka music grabbed his arm and pulled him to the middle of the tavern where she began taking high, rhythmic steps, locking elbows with Frank and sending the two in orbit around each other, bumping into tables and chairs so often that their clattering seemed to be part of the song.

A plump and pretty woman quickly grabbed Stan and joined in the dance. Soon the entire bar was polka-ing.

"This is our night!" Stan shouted to Frank.

Yes, it is, thought Frank, the whiskey pulling his blood through his heart and filling his mind with a total awareness of life, as if his body were the very accordion that was storming through his head.

The song ended and another began.

"'The Purple Polka' is my favorite," the woman said, pointing to her outfit as if she had planned the entire scene, unaware that her relationship with "The Purple Polka" was about to change forever.

As Frank prayed in rhythm to the dance, giving thanks for the blessings of his new son, his lovely little girl, and his wonderful wife, his heart began to pump faster, harder, trying to keep pace with the joy, but in the end it failed, failed completely, and in the middle of "The Purple Polka," Frank crashed to the floor.

An ambulance was quickly dispatched from the very building that housed Frank's son and wife who slept soundly, unaware of the turn their lives were taking. It took less than two minutes for the ambulance to arrive at The Lucky Harpoon, but when the paramedics entered between the ceramic mermaids, they found that there was nothing they could do. As they carried Frank's body from the tavern, Stan Noffsinger sat slumped against the bar as the lavender woman yanked the needle from "The Saturday Morning Polka."

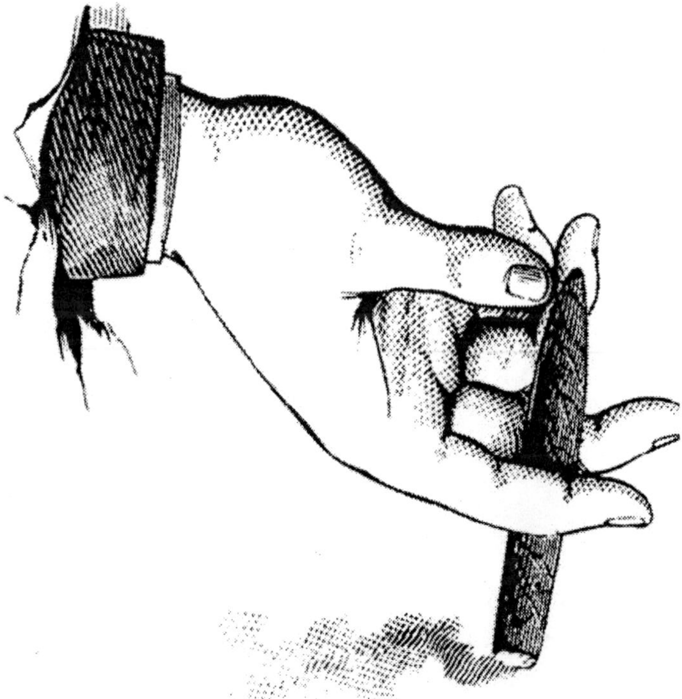

Unfortunately for Duke Stubbins and Decky Peteman we must now return to present day Midford, Ohio, where Roy and Talvin, the burly furniture movers, raise their large, coverall-clad bodies from the floor of the Crossroads Tavern.

The dendrites of Duke Stubbins's brain that had just moments ago received signals to form a fist and punch Roy, now receive this message: A lifetime of moving furniture probably makes one quite strong…and mean, too.

The fight messages quickly are replaced by flight messages, but not soon enough.

In a flash, Duke finds himself rising about a foot off of the ground, his neck wedged between Talvin's vise-like grip. A few gasps of air exit his mouth, but very little air makes its way back in. Just before Duke blacks out, he sees Roy send Decky Peteman flying across the barroom with a turbo-boosted uppercut.

By the time Molly Rendale returns from the kitchen with a tray of clean mugs, Duke has completely lost consciousness.

Molly Rendale is a large woman, not much smaller

than the brutish furniture movers. Her hair is shaved to within half an inch of her skull, and on her left shoulder is a half-dollar-sized tattoo of a black widow.

Molly is fond of only two people in the entire world. One is her lover, Phyllis Linski, a Barbie look-alike and the most prominent realtor in Midford; and the other is Duke Stubbins, who has drunk mutely at her bar every day for three decades.

The sight of Duke dangling from the out-of-towner's grip sends a river of rage flowing through Molly who delivers a swift kick to the man's groin and then smashes one of the glass mugs over his head as he doubles over, producing a deep cut along his brow.

Roy receives the same treatment, only reversed. First Molly shatters a mug over his skull and then finishes him off with a kick between the legs.

As Duke's breathing returns, Decky Peteman slowly comes into focus. Seeing Decky lying on the floor with a relieved grin on his face brings back the image of a much younger Decky laughing nervously after his balsa wings had delivered him unharmed from his fall from the trees during Duke's fathers' final masquerade party.

Duke says a prayer to the Oak Goddess, thanking her for sending Molly to deliver them safely from the fight. It is the first time he has prayed to her in almost thirty years.

Back home, Duke finds Novella Lee waiting for him at the front door. She runs to Duke and clasps his cheeks in her large, dark hands, examining his face and body. "Oh, Duke! What in the world did you get yourself into? Molly Rendale just called me to see if you were doing okay. Said you'd been in a bit of a fight."

Duke nods, enjoying the warmth of Novella Lee's hands against his face.

"Well, you get upstairs and take yourself a nice long shower."

Duke nods again and makes his way up the stairs (16 steps). In the bathroom Duke undresses slowly. His stretched neck has become quite sore, making it very difficult for him to remove his shirt and sweater.

After his shower, Duke and Novella Lee sit down to a dinner of roast pork, cabbage, garlic potatoes, and biscuits. Novella Lee hands Duke a small glass dish containing several dollops of jam. "I want you to try this, Duke. It's a new flavor we're trying: Pineapple Passion Fruit."

In his will, Marve Stubbins had named Novella Lee as president of Stubbins Jams. Her first inclination had been to decline the position, thinking she had little interest in the jelly world, but she gave it a few months and soon found herself enthusiastically immersed in the running of the company.

"Duke, I've been thinking. You're a special soul. There's no doubt about that. And there's something you've been looking for in that silence of yours, and I'm just not sure you're ever going to find it here in Midford. Now, your fathers left the two of us with more money than we'll ever be able to spend, and I think you should use some of it to get out and see the world."

The idea both excites and frightens Duke. It's true, he is searching, is on a constant quest for meaning, but the idea of looking beyond the confines of Midford makes Duke anxious.

"Your Pappa always spoke fondly of London. I think that might be a good place for you to start. You don't have to decide right now. You think about it and just let me know when you make up your mind."

After dinner Duke takes a walk in the backyard, his mind filled with images about what the world might look like beyond Midford. His head is busy with magazine images of London and Paris. Africa and Australia. The Taj Mahal. The Great Wall of China. Lions, koalas, and polar bears.

Duke plops to his knees beneath the largest tree in the woods. For the second time today, he prays silently to the Oak Goddess. If I should go, please give me a sign, he asks of Her.

Duke waits, but receives no sign. Maybe next year, he tells himself, rising to his feet and heading back towards the house.

Duke has taken less than five steps when a gust of wind moves through the calm air. A large limb at the top of the oak tree is dislodged by the gust and crashes to the ground in the exact spot where Duke had been kneeling only seconds earlier.

Duke takes this as his sign. London it is.

As the Rumpkins back down the drive, Sissy Rumpkin winces at the sight of Myron and Bambi standing in her lawn. She instructs Ted Rumpkin to stop the car.

"We've just had the lawn sprayed, so you really shouldn't stay out here any longer than you have to," she calls from her window. "And you can put the motorcycle in the garage. I'd feel awful if anything happened to it while you're doing us this favor."

Duke and Novella Lee are driven to the Midford airfield in the company limousine. The Midford airfield is little more than a cow pasture with a windsock. The only craft that flies out of the airfield is Stubbins Jam's small twin-engine plane piloted by Nix Calder, a corpulent middle-aged man with a pre-pubescent face.

Nix Calder descends the four stairs from the plane's doorway and greets Novella Lee and Duke. "Beautiful day for flying," he says with a broad smile.

"Well, it sure is," concurs Novella Lee. "I wish I was coming along with y'all."

You can go in my place, thinks Duke. The sight of the plane has made him quite nervous. He thinks of his fathers and how they must have felt during their final seconds.

Nix grabs Duke's suitcase and heads back up the stairs, but Duke does not follow.

"I'll miss you, Duke. Please write as often as you can," says Novella Lee as she gently shoves Duke towards the plane. Fourteen reluctant steps later, Duke is strapped in his seat and on his way.

At the Charlotte airport, Ted Rumpkin pulls the luggage from the back seat and comes across what appears to be an empty suitcase. "What is this?" he asks his wife, to which she replies, "It's an empty suitcase. You know I always take an extra suitcase to bring back anything we might buy."

"This is not a shopping trip! Do you realize how

much we've spent already!" he exclaims, tugging the suitcase back into the car. Sissy Rumpkin's knees buckle, and she finds herself sitting cross-legged on the asphalt, crying loudly.

Five minutes later Ted Rumpkin says, "Okay, we can take the damn suitcase," which Sissy Rumpkin grabs from the back seat herself, thankful that her husband has not noticed the rattling of the smaller empty suitcase nested inside.

On Saturday morning Myron wakes in the Rumpkin master bedroom, mildly hung over, his beard braided into strands of macramé. He vaguely remembers Bambi performing this artwork just before he fell into a deep, drunken sleep. Between him and Bambi lie Stonewall and Lee, still damp from their play in the hot tub.

Myron stabs a button on the remote control and John Wayne pops onto the big screen television. Myron and Bambi spend the morning watching old movies, leaving the bed only for an occasional trip to the liquor cabinet to combat their hangovers. It's vacation time, after all.

The Rumpkins sit at Kennedy Airport, delayed by a late spring snowstorm. Sissy Rumpkin squints in concentration, willing the snow to melt, while Ted Rumpkin prays for more winter weather.

Duke's fear has been run off by his excitement. The Stubbins' company airplane is but a small insect compared to the mammoth machines that fill the runways of Kennedy Airport. Duke's flight to London has been delayed, but he is content to walk the corridors. He senses a sort of energy that he has never felt in Midford.

Duke is thinking, Perhaps the Oak Goddess has steered me correctly, and maybe meaning is on the horizon, when his flight is finally announced over the intercom.

While Bambi examines Ted Rumpkin's gun case, home to over a dozen shotguns, Myron dances around the kitchen preparing an early afternoon brunch. Drunkenness has sent his hangover packing.

As Myron places the last slices of Swiss cheese on his and Bambi's sandwiches, he is distracted by a bumblebee buzzing outside the window. A banker he once met at a bar told Myron that the bumblebee is the sole clue to the punch line of the Cosmic Joke.

According to the banker, there isn't an engineer in the world who can explain how a bumblebee flies. The laws of dynamics forbid the bumblebee to defeat gravity. If Newton had been stung by a bee rather than whacked by an apple, he would not have made the slightest dent in the history of physics. According to the banker, the bumblebee is the one clue left behind by the Creator to let us in on the nature of his absurd existential experiment.

Cecil Leadman, driving his VW Beetle that is cleaner than it was when it rolled off the assembly line in the early 70's, makes a right turn into a subdivision marked by a large, stone-bordered sign which bears the name "Pine Lake."

When he last left the Pine Lake neighborhood, its streets had been studded with yellow fliers, but as he drives down Long-Leaf Drive, he sees not one flier still tacked to a mailbox. Ditto on Loblolly Lane. But his spirits rise when he turns onto Spruce Way and spots one of the yellow flags flying from the mailbox of a large, white three-story. Upon further evaluation, however, Cecil rejects the house, deeming it too well-lit with high street visibility. He decides to break for lunch.

As Stonewall and Lee clean up the leftovers from brunch, Myron asks Bambi how she'd feel about a motorcycle ride. Already feeling the vibrations between her legs, Bambi responds with an enthusiastic, "You betcha!"

Before mounting the bike, Myron strokes his beard, takes a deep breath, and pontificates, "When it was born in 1981, the Seca 750 was more bike than the roads had ever seen. We've both gotten a lot older since then, but we're both still a helluva lot of fun."

The speech is beautiful to Bambi. She thinks it sounds literary, making Myron seem large and timeless, like the men from the dusty texts of her high school English classes. She feels moved by Myron's words, despite the fact that she's heard the same speech at least twice a week, ever since it first came to Myron several years ago.

Myron mounts the motorcycle and slides his black, full-faced helmet over his head, giving him a resemblance to Darth Vader. Then he pulls on a pair of fingerless, black leather gloves, raises his visor, and as he offers Bambi her small, white helmet he says, "Would the lady care for a ride?"

Bambi dons her helmet, the plastic dome coming to

rest just above her ears. Myron wishes she would wear a full helmet for better protection. "That face of yours is a national treasure, and it's your duty to this country to protect it," he once told her. But if there's one thing Myron holds dear, it's freedom, and besides that, Bambi's rhetorical skills had made a formidable appearance as she argued, "What better way to show the public their treasure, than parading it through town on the back of your motorcycle?... Besides, if we wreck, my heart will stop before I hit the ground."

In London, the Rumpkins walk into the lobby of the Travilly, the magnificent five-star hotel where they are to spend the next seven days. Upon entering, Sissy Rumpkin thinks, "What a magnificent shopping headquarters," and Ted Rumpkin thinks, "Not a bad place to die."

Myron and Bambi pull into the entrance of Pickett Park and dismount. While Myron unstraps the "moto-rang," a small boomerang he keeps strapped to the side of the motorcycle, Bambi heads over to the swingset and chooses the middle of the three swings.

With a few strong pumps of her legs she is soaring, so that at the apex of her flight her head is even with the crossbar of the swing set.

Across the playground, a mother supervises her small son and smaller daughter as they play on the slide. The boy has removed his shoes and attempts to run up the slide in sock feet. Bambi transforms this image into scenes for an infomercial for The Sock Jogger.

On the other side of the park, Myron stands in a small field throwing his boomerang into a steady breeze and smoking one of Ted Rumpkin's cigars.

"What is it about you and boomerangs?" Bambi had asked Myron when they first started seeing each other.

"Within each boomerang lies the great Tao, and if one can access the Tao and let it run through the body, through the soul, then the result will be a perfect toss, and the boomerang will return to the thrower as easily as the seasons return to the earth," Myron answered as Bambi realized she was falling in love.

Once in London, Duke Stubbins was to check into the Linton Hotel, but instead he walked for miles around the streets of London (4,675 steps). The sight of strange new sidewalks had thrown Duke's feet into a Dionysian frenzy which, unfortunately, yielded no

smoke and gravity

trace of meaning.

Thoroughly exhausted, Duke now hands the desk clerk at the Linton a list of written instructions from Novella Lee.

"I hope you'll enjoy your stay, sir," says the clerk.

If Duke were the speaking type he would answer, "I'm sure I will. You have incredible sidewalks."

His lunch break over, Cecil Leadman now directs his Volkswagen Beetle into the Timber Haven subdivision. It is not until the last house of the back-most street that he comes across a flier still flapping from a mailbox. It is the home where the woman had chased the man around the yard with her breasts. What a perfect house it is: back from the street, low traffic, and poor outside lighting.

Cecil steers his Volkswagen home with the satisfaction of a successful day's work.

Myron heaves his small boomerang hard and low, sending it into a double loop. At the end of the second loop, the "moto-rang" rises and sails over his head, landing near the sock-footed boy who is still struggling to make his way up the shiny metal slide.

"That was cool, Mister," says the boy, jumping down from the slide to hand the boomerang to Myron. Myron is startled; the boy is the spitting image of Josh Marino, the son of a bank president and cosmetics entrepreneur for whom Myron had built a scale replica of the Leaning Tower of Pisa around an eighty foot elm tree. It was a twenty-thousand dollar project, Myron's biggest ever at the time.

"Can I try it?" asks the small boy.

"Sure. Let's go give it a shot," says Myron, looking at the boy's mother for consent which she gladly gives.

"My name's Timmy," says the boy.

"A fine name," Myron assures him.

While Timmy tosses the boomerang around the small field, Myron recalls the seven weeks he spent building Josh Marino's Tower of Pisa around the leaning elm. For almost two months he worked on the immaculate grounds surrounding the Marinos' four-story house without running into the owners a single time. A few times toward the end, after he'd run the power and installed lights throughout the eight tiers, he'd worked late enough to see Jane Marino come home with Josh in the evening, but when Josh would try to break free of her grip to take a look at his new play palace, his mother would yank him toward the house. "Come on, Josh. Let's leave the busy man alone," she'd say.

Myron thought that it was ironic that the Marinos probably spent thousands of dollars a month on a home which they seemed to use only for sleep. He got to be good friends with the gardener, Patrick, an ancient Irishman who was usually the only other person around. Sometimes they'd have lunch together underneath the large gazebo in the rose garden.

And then one Friday Myron climbed to the top tier to finish the interior trim and found Josh sitting quietly on the floor, staring out the window up into the dense, green foliage.

"Shouldn't you be in school?" Myron asked.

"Shouldn't you be finished by now?" the boy countered. "My mom says you're probably an alcoholic or something and that you probably only work an hour or two a day on this thing."

Myron was taken aback by the boy referring to his masterpiece as "this thing." He'd spent nearly a hundred hours in the library researching Pisa's famous tower before he anchored the first timber to the old elm, and as far as his work habits, Myron knew there were few people who could finish a project of this size within a year, much less two months.

"I'm sure your mother's a very smart woman," Myron said flatly, measuring a piece of trim board to go above the door.

"Then why does she think I'm in school right now?"

"She probably trusts you. Nothing wrong with that, is there?"

"If she trusts me, then why doesn't she ever let me do what I want to?"

"What is it that you want to do?"

"I don't know. I never get a chance to find out."

"Why not?"

"Lessons."

"What kind of lessons?"

"You name it, I do it. Piano, tennis, golf, sailing."

"Sounds pretty fun to me."

"Sometimes. But today's the worst."

"What's today?" asked Myron.

"Chess."

Myron enjoys chess himself, but he understood how someone Josh's age (Myron guessed no older than ten) might not care for the game.

"What don't you like about chess?" Myron asked.

"Losing."

"No one likes losing."

"That's what my father says. He yells at me when I lose. He says life is about winning."

Myron mentally cussed Josh's father. "Life's about a lot of things," he said, placing the trim board on his miter saw and cutting it at forty-five degrees.

"What do you think life's about?" Josh asked above the noise, resuming his gaze out of the window.

Quite a question to come from a ten-year old,

thought Myron. He decided to give it his best shot. "I don't like to give advice, but here's how I see it. If life's a forest, some people spend their entire lives standing beside an elm tree. This happens to be an elm tree, by the way," Myron said, nodding to the thick trunk that stabbed through the center of the room.

"I know," Josh snapped back without breaking his gaze out of the window.

"Anyway, people who spend their whole lives by an elm tree say life's an elm forest. Other people spend their lives beside an oak, and they say life's an oak forest. And then you have your maple people, your pine people, and so on. There seems to be a good amount of tension between these different groups. Of course, some people can see that the forest is made up of elms, oaks, pines, maples, poison ivy, mushrooms, moss, and vines, but, I far as I can tell, these people tend to catch hell from everyone."

Josh turned from the window to look at Myron. "What kind of person are you?"

"Me? I try to stay out of it. I just want my own little clearing in the woods so I can make it whatever I want it to be. If I can have that, people can call the woods whatever they damn well please."

Josh smiled. He liked Myron's use of profanity. "I know what you mean. Sometimes I want to burn the whole fucking woods," he said, over-emphasizing 'fucking.'

Josh and Myron chatted the rest of the afternoon, Myron letting Josh fumble with the tape measurer and slam nails into some of the less delicate trim work. Myron knocked off early to avoid the drama that would surely ensue once Josh was found to be AWOL from chess practice.

"Mister, this thing must be broke," says the Josh-look-alike in Pickett Park as he brushes off the dirt that clings to the boomerang after being pulled from the small divot it created in the red soil. "It ain't coming back at all."

"Let me see if I can fix it," Myron says, pretending to make some adjustments. As Myron makes a near perfect toss, he feels the slightest of tears warming the bottom of his eyes. The day after his talk with Josh, the Marinos drove to Maryland where Josh won his first regional chess tournament. On the way home, his father fell asleep at the wheel and the Marinos were all killed instantly when they crossed over the median and collided with an oncoming Volvo.

Myron gives the boomerang to the boy and calls Bambi, giving her a gentle kiss before they strap on their helmets and rumble down the road.

Back in London, the Rumpkins have made it to their room. Sissy Rumpkin removes her clothes and climbs into bed, holding a mental pep rally to prepare for sex with Ted Rumpkin.

The pep rally is happily cancelled when Ted Rumpkin plops into bed and, within minutes, begins producing world-class snores.

Though it is only late afternoon in Pickett, Cecil Leadman is sound asleep on the crisp white sheets of his single bed. His alarm clock is set for one a.m.

Myron and Bambi return to the Rumpkin house with four large ribeye steaks, which Bambi has clutched under one arm while she clings to Myron with the other.

Once back at the Rumpkin house, Myron goes to the back deck to light the grill. Why four steaks instead of two? Myron and Bambi have invited Stonewall and Lee to dinner.

And now we wait on the clock to move us ahead into our story.

While we wait, let's check in on a dream that is being dreamt by Duke. He dreams of a large oak tree, which within the span of a handful of synapses in his sleeping brain, becomes animated, developing arms, a face, and a pleasant, knowing voice.

It has been said that an account of another person's dream is among the most boring of activities, and for this reason we will not examine Duke's dream any further, but I have a feeling that if we could look ahead to what tomorrow holds, we might find a certain relevance to his dream of a talking tree.

Myron, Bambi, Stonewall, and Lee now lie fast asleep on the bed in the Rumpkins' guest bedroom, having found the master bed still a bit damp.

All four sleep soundly, pleasantly stuffed with red meat. Myron and Bambi, being also full of gin, do not react whatsoever to the rustling that makes its way from behind the house up to the bedroom, but the ears belonging to the sleeping Stonewall and Lee give a slight twitch.

Within minutes, the rustling gives way to a loud crash. This, too, falls mutely to the human ears, but the cacophony jerks the Irish Setters from their dreams of cow meat and sends them dancing around the bed.

Meanwhile, in London, the sun has already crept upon the scene. Ted Rumpkin remains in bed, dreaming a bizarre dream involving Linda Coxdale's breasts and Dr. Kavorkian, but Sissy Rumpkin has already left the Travilly with her two empty suitcases, and sits outside of Harrods. It will be three minutes before the department store opens its doors.

During these same three minutes, Cecil Leadman carefully slides through the frame of the Rumpkins' garage window, which lies shattered on the cement floor below him. He feels his way across the garage and finds the door to the house.

With any occupation, there are small things that can make a big difference. A waiter occasionally runs across patrons in the habit of tipping extravagantly. A plumber might arrive at a sink to find that all it needs is to have chicken gristle removed from its neck. The elementary school student is sometimes treated to a day of filmstrips. And sometimes the burglar runs across a house ready to be burgled, thinks Cecil Leadman, as he turns the doorknob and finds it unlocked.

During these three minutes, Stonewall and Lee manage to lick Bambi into consciousness. Bambi, hearing noises downstairs, attempts to wake Myron, but even when she shakes him firmly by the shoulders, he does not awaken from his drunken slumber.

The doors to Harrods swing open and Sissy Rumpkin dives in, immersing herself in silk, gold, and precious stones, wondering if she'll run out of room in her suitcases before she runs out of room on her credit cards.

Duke also walks through Harrods. So far today he has taken over five thousand steps without finding even a trace of meaning.

Myron dreams. In his dream he is in his backyard, surrounded by Irish Setters, hundreds of them. The sky is full of boomerangs.

Myron wears a large white robe. A falcon sits on his shoulder. Bambi enters his dream and crawls beneath the robe, finding his cock with her mouth.

As Myron's penis becomes firmer, blood exits his dreaming brain and he gradually fades into wakefulness. Bambi is the only element that remains from the dream.

"Mmmmmmm. That feels…"

Bambi jumps out of bed, grabs Myron's arms, and pulls him to his feet. "I think someone's downstairs!" she explains in a whispered shout, gently shoving Myron towards the bedroom door. He exits the room with his erection pointing the way.

A diamond pendant sits in its glass case in Harrods as it has for three months. Thousands of years ago the diamond had lived the dark life of a lump of coal, trapped beneath tons of earth without any knowledge that such a thing as sunlight even existed. During these dark years it learned humility, selflessness, and stillness. And by the time it found itself transformed into its current brilliance, it had mastered the spiritual energies: the Tao, the Chi, the Holy Groove.

So now it sits in the glass case, collecting the energy of the universe, focusing this energy within itself, and emitting it ten-fold back into the world in the form of invisible rays of its diamond soul.

Sissy Rumpkin is unaware that it is these rays of diamond soul that have led her past the tempting shoes, silk blouses, and luxurious leather handbags. She thinks she is merely taking a warm-up lap around the store, trying to clear her head of her outside life so she can give a worthy shopping performance. But as she passes the glass case, the nerves of her skin tingle as if she has just walked through a spider web. She drops the suitcases and turns to the diamond.

Ted Rumpkin has not left the hotel room. He lies on the bed pondering creative methods of suicide. So far he has come up with three possibilities:
1) He could fill one of the glasses from the bathroom with water, place it on the bed between two pillows, and then lie face down over it, squeezing his mouth and nose into the water until he drowns.
2) He could lie on the floor in front of the television, raise his legs, tie the television's power cord around his ankles, and then lower his legs to cause the television to crash down on him.
3) He could zip himself in a clothing bag and puff on cigarettes until he dies of smoke inhalation.

Ted Rumpkin finds none of these options tempting, so he continues searching for possibilities as he thinks back to his adolescent years when he dreamed of being a famous actor, living only for the camera and his fans. Whatever happened to that dream, he asks himself.

He recalls the weeks he spent during his senior year of high school immersed in his role as Willy Loman in *Death of a Salesman*. The long hours of rehearsal passed quickly as he struggled along with Willie Loman to find satisfaction in the world. A week into the role, he felt himself actually becoming Willie Loman. During algebra class he would feel guilty as he studied Angela Newberry who played Linda, his on-stage wife. As Angela scribbled away at quadratic formulas, Ted would yearn to find a way to help Willie Loman get a better grasp on reality so that he could repair the havoc he was wreaking on the Loman family. Sometimes Angela would turn and smile at him, and he could only feel remorse for his unfaithfulness to his loving wife and shame for his role in their sons' unhappiness.

As sometimes happens in the theatre, Ted found himself falling for the leading lady. He wasn't sure whether his attraction stemmed from the love and compassion Linda Loman offered him on stage or whether it was due to Angela Newberry's good looks and slightly rebellious bent. Angela's father was a retired naval officer and Angela had spent most of her childhood in Europe, giving her an air of worldliness that set her apart from the other students at Drysdale High.

One night after rehearsal, Angela asked Ted if he wanted to go out to the practice fields and share a bottle of bourbon she'd pilfered from her father.

"I'm glad we're in the play together," Angela told Ted as she gave him the bottle of bourbon to hold as she spread out an old wool blanket she'd brought along.

"Me too," said Ted, twisting the bottle open and letting the dusky aroma drift into his nostrils. Though alcohol was the source of the fortune left to his family by his grandfather, Ted had never taken a single drink.

Ted sat down beside Angela, handed her the bottle, and watched as she casually tipped the bottle up, swallowed, wiped her mouth, and handed the bottle back.

"I don't think I care for any right now. Thanks."

"But I thought that's why we came out here," Angela pointed out, drawing her face into a question mark.

Ted laughed. "Just kidding," he said, incorporating the charm Willy Loman had perfected in his constant pursuit of approval and popularity. He put the bottle to his lips and took an aggressive chug in an effort to impress Angela.

Ted felt the bourbon burn and swell in the back of his throat, and instead of making its way down his esophagus, it erupted out of his mouth, dousing Angela's skirt.

"Well, I guess that will make it easier for Pop to figure out what happened to his bourbon," she said good-naturedly.

"I'm so sorry," Ted said, pulling off his shirt and using it in a futile attempt to dry Angela's skirt.

"Don't worry about it," she said, but as he tried to put his shirt back on she grabbed his arms and unabashedly studied Ted's chest, his muscles full and firm from four years on the Drysdale crew team. "You should keep your shirt off. The air feels great tonight, doesn't it?"

"Yeah, it does," Ted agreed meekly, still embarrassed about his bourbon eruption.

"Don't drink it like a soda," Angela instructed. "Throw it back fast and swallow it all at once." She demonstrated her technique and gave the bottle back to Ted who followed her instructions as best he could and managed to get a swallow down without wetting Angela any further. As the sting of the bourbon dissipated, Ted enjoyed the warmth it left behind.

The next few swigs went down progressively more

smoothly and Ted felt himself growing lighter as if the bourbon were somehow erasing gravity.

"You're a good actor," Angela said.

"You, too."

"That Willy Loman's quite an ass, isn't he?"

"I don't think he means to be," Ted responded somewhat defensively as if Angela were criticizing him and not the character he was playing. "The world's just different than he wants it to be."

"Well now, isn't that unusual," Angela said sarcastically. "Do you know anyone who wouldn't like the world to be different than it is?"

Ted laughed at himself. "I suppose there must be someone who enjoys the greed, chaos, and violence."

"Yeah, but the flowers and puppy dogs probably tick them off," Angela said, wrapping her hands around Ted's and pulling the bourbon bottle to her mouth. When she released her grasp, Ted enjoyed the heated imprint where her hands had meshed with his. As he took another drink, the external chill of the autumn air combined with the warmth of the bourbon, and the excitement of being alone under the stars with Angela was creating a thrill that was moving out of control.

Without even knowing he was going to say it, he looked at Angela and said, "I'd really like to kiss you."

"Excuse me?" Angela responded, unalarmed.

A panic set in over Ted. Self-awareness returned

with a heavy thud. He turned from Angela and looked to the stars for help. "Oh, nothing."

"Thanks a lot. It's an honor knowing that you consider the idea of kissing me to be nothing."

"That's not what I meant," stammered Ted.

"Then what did you mean?"

"I just shouldn't have said anything. That's all."

"Why not?" Angela pushed.

"I don't know." Ted's discomfort was swelling.

"Did you mean it?"

"I guess so."

"But you're not sure?"

"It's no big deal," Ted said, still not looking at Angela. "Let's just drop it."

"Ted, can I tell you something?" Angela asked, sweeping her hair behind her shoulders.

"Go ahead."

"I'm sure."

"Sure of what?"

"I'm sure I'd like for you to kiss me."

Ted's anxiety vanished. He turned to Angela and the kiss took care of itself as if they'd rehearsed it a hundred times.

After several minutes of sharing their bourbon-flavored mouths, Angela smiled at Ted. "Are you sure, yet?"

Angela helped Ted free her from her bra and as his mouth surrounded the flesh of her breasts Ted felt a wonderful urgency build throughout his body. He fumbled through his wallet and pulled out a condom in a faded wrapper which he had carried for months with a vague hopefulness that it would one day be put to use.

Ted fought to free the condom from the wrapper until Angela finally took it from him, unwrapped it, and unrolled it over his concrete erection as Ted watched in disbelief, trying to fathom the fact that at any moment he was going to enter the body of another human being.

At home later, Ted would spend hours reliving Angela's hands guiding him inside her. At first he wasn't sure what to do next, but when she thrust her hips to let him in even deeper, he thrust back and soon they were rocking in a wonderful rhythm, and Ted felt all of the emotion and energy of the night's events gather in his groin.

The urgency of his thrusts, his explosive heart beat, and his virginal ecstasy were finally too much to contain, and Ted felt the world gather at the tip of his cock and then explode.

As he lay on top of Angela, still inside her, the sweat on his back began to dry in the soft breeze and he found himself once again not knowing what to do, but now there was less discomfort in not knowing. Angela smiled gently as she rolled him over slowly, twitching slightly with discomfort as he slid out of her.

Ted stared into the sky, fully contented, and feeling the moment called for him to say something, he whispered appreciatively into Angela's ear, "Thank you," to which Angela responded with laughter and a gentle kiss on the cheek.

Ted spent much of that night staring at himself in the mirror to see if he could notice any changes, searching for physical markings of his new non-virginity and wondering what he should feel, wondering what Angela was feeling.

He was surprised and disappointed the next day in algebra class when things seemed to be business as usual between himself and Angela, friendly and warm, but no acknowledgement of the previous night's monumental event. For the rest of the day he felt an underlying apprehension, afraid that his assumption that he and Angela would repeat their sexual escapade had been erroneous.

Ted went to rehearsal early hoping to arrive before Angela, but when he entered the auditorium he found her sitting with a small group of other cast and crew members engaged in easy conversation.

"No way in hell anybody's going to beat the Cardinals," announced Hoite Connelly in a squeaky voice that seemed appropriate for his diminutive frame. Hoite was the lighting technician for the show.

"No way in hell anyone in their right mind gives a damn," Angela teased Hoite, giving his shoulder a playful shove. Ted knew it was ridiculous, but he resented Hoite for being touched by Angela.

"Angela's right. Baseball's an anachronism," said Baryd Rinkle who played Biff, one of Ted's on-stage sons. "All sports are a throwback to the Neanderthal days." Hoite was about to object, but Angela asked to hear more about Baryd's theory. "It's really quite obvious. Thousands of years ago we worshipped the tribal member who could throw a stone the farthest and most accurately. If our fellow clansman, let's call him Grunt, if Grunt could hurl a rock at a fleeing Gostradom fifty paces away and strike it in the skull, if Grunt could outrun the stunned animal, if Grunt was pumped with enough testosterone to wrestle the wild beast to the ground and pound it dead with his fist, then we all wanted Grunt to like us. We studied Grunt. We wanted to know everything about Grunt. We wanted to be Grunt, but if we couldn't be Grunt we at least wanted Grunt to like us enough to share his catch. So now, whether we admit it or not, even though the local grocer has stripped Grunt of his societal role, many of us are still hard-wired to worship the perfection of Neanderthal skills, and so we pack ourselves together and root for our team to win the hunt."

"I think you're on to something," Angela said to

Baryd, "but I think the Neanderthals did a number of things we still like to do." Angela punctuated her sentence with a glance in Ted's direction, sending his heart asputter.

"And I happen to find baseball more interesting than cave paintings," Hoite said defensively.

As Ted was relishing Angela's acknowledgment of the previous night's communion, Mr. Bernstein appeared on the stage and instructed everyone to take their places for rehearsal of the final scene.

"I find cave painting quite enjoyable, myself," Ted said as he walked to the stage.

Rehearsal did not go well. While Angela easily slid into her role of Linda Loman, Ted could not transform into her life-battered, worn out husband still clinging to illusions he knew no longer existed.

"Cut, cut," called Mr. Bernstein. "Willy (Mr. Bernstein always addressed the cast by their character names), you're supposed to be distant, not glowing. Dreamy, but not radiant. Remember, within the next hour you're going to kill yourself."

But no matter how hard he tried, Ted could not become a disenchanted, exhausted man. The idea of death had been pushed far out of his reach as his mind swirled with enough endorphins to power the town of Pickett for a decade.

After nearly an hour of futile attempts to guide

his Willy Loman toward despair or anything even approaching dissatisfaction, Mr. Bernstein called it quits for the night, instructing Ted to find some way to make himself less happy before the following day's rehearsal.

"We need to talk," Angela said as they left the stage. "Let's take a walk."

Angela led Ted down the hall and out of the side doors by the shop classroom where she sat him down on a sawhorse and addressed him sternly. "You have to stop."

"Stop what?" Ted asked, his happiness waning rapidly as the back of his mind translated for him Angela's tone. Whatever was coming would not be good.

"You're falling in love with me, and you have to stop."

Falling in love. Ted hadn't verbalized it, hadn't thought about it in specific terms. He only knew that for twenty-four hours his mind had been incapable of manipulating any information that didn't pertain in one way or other to Angela Newberry. "I don't want to stop," he informed her.

"You don't have a choice."

How could he not have a choice, Ted wondered. After all, it was his mind, and if there were any matter in which he had no choice it was the fact that his brain had been short-circuited by the awareness that Ted's body had entered Angela's body and all that mattered in the entire world was that it happen again as soon as possible. A kiss or even interwoven fingers would suffice, but his brain was demanding that in some manner they come together and stay that way for an indefinite period of time.

"I'm sorry, Ted. You just can't fall in love with me." Angela's face was distorted by sternness or by a futile attempt to suppress her attractiveness. "I like you a lot, and last night was a good time, better than a good time. It was great, but it can't happen again."

"But why?" Ted pleaded, tears beginning to form as Angela's demands became more and more real to him.

"Because I'm falling in love with you, too."

"Then there's no problem."

"There's a huge problem. I should have told you before, but I had no way of knowing it mattered. We're moving after this semester. My father's bored with retirement, and he's taking some stupid job in San Francisco."

"What kind of job?" Ted asked because in his panic he could think of no better response.

"Something to do with advertising, but that's beside the point. You just have to stop falling in love with me."

Ted reached out for Angela, but she backed away.

"But why?"

"I just told you why."

"You just told me you were moving, but I don't see what that has to do with anything."

"It has everything to do with everything. Look, no matter what you think about it now, it will hurt too much later. We just have to stop things right here."

Ted's chest ached. He could feel his sternum trying to crack open. Nothing Angela had said made sense to him. He searched for the words that would make everything right, make Angela withdraw her demand. "Just let me kiss you," he begged.

Angela ignored his request. "I'm telling you, Ted, you just have to stop," and with that she turned and walked back inside while Ted sat on the sawhorse for several minutes and tried not to cry.

"Jesus Christ!" bellowed Mr. Bernstein. "Don't you do anything half-way?" Ted had gone from being a too radiant Willy Loman to a lifeless lump. "Now I can't even believe you have the energy to get in the car and kill yourself. When you're supposedly hoeing the garden, please try moving the hoe, Mr. Loman."

But once again Mr. Bernstein was forced to capitulate to Ted's emotions and end practice early. Ted's heart was blocking his mind. The lines he'd had down perfectly for weeks were suddenly inaccessible. His limbs were heavy, and whatever energy he managed to summon was quickly spent trying to fall out of love or plotting a strategy to convince Angela to allow him to remain in love.

As the days passed Ted's condition improved, or perhaps it would be more accurate to say that it became more manageable. He was gradually learning to let the darkest parts of himself fall away from the rest of his being. He began to feel like a small but functioning version of himself dragging around a bag of heaviness he dare not open.

By the time the show opened, Ted had once again gained access to his lines and his bag of heaviness had actually drawn him closer to Willy Loman. It occurred to Ted that all Willy Loman wanted was to love the world, but the more he tried, the more the world said "no."

It didn't take long for Ted to get past the shock of realizing the auditorium was full of people. It was only a matter of minutes before he became unaware of the dozen or so Rumpkins who sat in the front row. All that mattered was Willy Loman's battle against the world he wanted to love, and Ted entered the battle at full speed, becoming more and more embittered by the inevitable outcome. By the final scene, Ted found himself immersed in Willy Loman's illusions, fully in agreement that reality was no place to live a life, and as Angela stood by, he felt his excitement grow. She would be there for his death, and in the end, she'd know how much he cared.

As Baryd Rinkle delivered Biff's departing words, Ted fell easily into excited tears before departing the stage and letting the others listen to his car drive him to his death.

The curtain dropped over his stage family at his graveside, and Ted felt a rush of energy as he realized what a fine performance he had given. While waiting for the roar of applause, he thanked Arthur Miller for writing such a wonderful play and for introducing him to Willy Loman.

But the thunderous applause never came. There was clapping, but it barely reached the mandatory volume of politeness. At first Ted thought that his intuition had been seriously off-track, that his performance must have been mediocre at best, but when he made his curtain call, he knew this was not the case. The audience was beyond enthused; they were stunned. He had given them a Willy Loman packed with sad truths, and even through the bright lights he saw in each dim face an appreciation for his having provided the dark comfort of knowing that they were not alone.

"Ted was right," thinks Sissy, "I don't need to fill two suitcases. In fact, I wouldn't need to shop anymore for months. All I need is that little diamond."

Actually, the diamond is not little. It is over three carats. Three carats that would shout to the world that Sissy Rumpkin is back, three carats that would show all of Pickett that Linda Coxdale's breasts may have slowed them down, but in the end, the Rumpkins have prevailed.

Sissy Rumpkin feels the rays of diamond soul move through her body and mistakes these rays for a message from God. She glows in the warmth of a world that has changed for the better.

Duke moves through Harrods, envious of those around him. If only the shoppers could teach him the magic of material things. Then he'd simply wire Novella Lee for thousands of pounds, francs, and dollars and the world would shine brightly.

Six time zones away, Myron moves down the hallway slowly, quietly placing each foot before lifting the other, much like Frank Fugate had years earlier as he ascended the rickety stairs to Francie's attic apartment.

One of Myron's steps falls upon a boomerang. Stonewall had found it earlier in the day when he was exploring Bambi's bag and decided the boomerang would provide a nice dental workout. Myron picks up the boomerang and continues down the hall.

Duke Stubbins passes between Sissy Rumpkin and the three-carat chi machine, temporarily blocking Sissy Rumpkin from the pure energy of the diamond soul rays.

In this brief moment, the darkest part of her mind seizes the opportunity and begins blasting the part of her brain that is trying to delude itself into happiness and well being.

"Look at the price," the dark part of her brain murmurs to its innocent neighbor. "He'll never buy it for you. He doesn't have the money. The well's run dry."

As the mustiness of the passing stranger wafts away, a great depression settles over Sissy. The diamond that could save her life is only a few feet away, having lived for eons below the earth to perfect its beauty, men having died in the diamond mines to unearth it, a craftsman having devoted his lifetime to the art of cutting and mounting magic, and now all she needs to do to make it hers is to hand over forty-five thousand dollars to a representative of the department store. All that life demands of her at this moment is a mere five figures on a piece of plastic or paper.

It is a demand she cannot meet, and Sissy Rumpkin drops to her knees in tears.

Duke turns to locate the sobs that have filled the air. He sees a woman slumped against a display case, pawing at a glass case housing a large diamond solitaire like a puppy wanting in from the cold.

Now that's passion, thinks Duke. That's appreciation. That's someone who understands beauty.

As Duke approaches the woman, he is bombarded by diamond soul rays. And, just as Sissy Rumpkin had minutes earlier, Duke mistakes the origin of the sudden energy and believes himself to be receiving, finally, a message from the goddess.

Duke places his right hand on the shoulder of the woman we know to be Sissy Rumpkin and whom Duke believes to be a holy messenger.

Sissy Rumpkin looks up at Duke and wonders why the man has rested his hand on her shoulder. Is he welcoming her to the world of poverty?

The woman's expression seems to demand a response, but Duke isn't sure whether that's possible. Is he still capable of voice? Exactly how is it one forces words from the mind into the air? Even if he can speak, what does one ask a goddess?

And then Duke utters his first word in nearly thirty years: "Why?"

It is the perfect choice of words with which to

reintroduce his vocal cords to the world of reverberation. "Why" flows deep and smooth along Duke's throat, a silky pillow of sound that waltzes gracefully from his mouth.

Duke thinks, Not so bad, if I do say so myself.

Why, thinks Sissy Rumpkin. Why? Why? Why? Why? Why? And then an image of Linda Coxdale forms in her mind. "You want to know why? I'll tell you why," she says to Duke, "because of two damn breasts." With this she rises and runs out of the store.

Duke is stunned with the anti-climax of such a bizarre response to his first utterance in three decades. What was the goddess telling him? Could the key to the world really be "two damn breasts"?

It just can't be, he tells himself. That would mean that the majority of teen-age boys know more about truth than the sum of philosophical history. Hundreds of questions flood his mind, but his messenger has fled.

Not knowing what else to do, he begins to walk. During his disappointing confrontation with Truth, he has lost track of his steps, so he is forced to restart his count.

One, two, three...

Go to the park and give someone a boomerang, and most likely he will throw it as he would a Frisbee, curling his arm around it and letting it fly from his mid-section. Once this happens, the boomerang can do nothing but climb skyward for a second or two and then dive at a great speed to the ground where it will most likely shatter into several splintered pieces.

Give a boomerang to a hungry aboriginal hunter and, upon spotting a small game animal within range, he will throw the boomerang in an overhand manner almost identical to that of a centerfielder launching a throw to home plate. The boomerang will either render the animal the evening meal, or it will swoosh past the fortunate animal, take three left turns, and return to the thrower for another chance.

When Myron happens upon Cecil Leadman in the Rumpkin's living room, his reflexes send his boomerang hurtling at the intruder.

Myron throws the boomerang like a hungry aboriginal hunter.

Imagine yourself becoming thirsty as you read this page. Picture yourself going into the kitchen, grabbing a glass from the cabinet, then opening the refrigerator to fill the glass with the beverage of your choice. What is your emotional state at this moment?

Now imagine opening the refrigerator to find a midget clown who springs into your kitchen and begins to juggle seventeen flaming chickens. This is exactly how Cecil Leadman feels as Myron lunges toward him with a howl and launches a boomerang at his skull.

The neighborhoods that Cecil Leadman preys upon are comprised of doctors and insurance executives. Here a college president, there an owner of a chain of muffler shops. But never a macramé-bearded wild man. Besides, when Cecil Leadman burgles a home, it's supposed to be empty. That's the rule.

In flight, a boomerang spins rapidly end over end, creating a circular image that looks like a translucent record album moving through space. As this airy disc flies towards his skull, cutting its way through the mad howl that has engulfed the room, Cecil Leadman's sole thought is this: The rules have been broken.

As Ted Rumpkin lies on the bed of his hotel, his sole thought is this: I don't really want to die. I simply want another life.

Walking back to the hotel, Sissy Rumpkin's sole thought is this: If I can't buy diamonds, I might as well be dead.

And Duke's sole thought is this: Two damn breasts? I just don't get it.

Sissy Rumpkin returns to the Travilly. As she enters the hotel room, she is furious at Ted Rumpkin for losing all of their money. She slams the door and takes a deep breath in preparation to lambaste her husband for his failures.

But the deep breath turns into a confused gasp. "What in the hell are you doing?" she asks her husband.

Ted Rumpkin does not answer. He is sitting on the floor with his legs crossed yogi-fashioned. He is wearing nothing but a white sheet wrapped loosely around his body.

"Have you lost your mind?" asks Sissy. She notices one of the windows open and crosses the room for a deep breath of fresh air, but as she leans out of the window she notices a puddle of color on the sidewalk below. Upon examination, she recognizes the puddle of color to be composed of clothing, and turning to notice an empty suitcase on the sheetless bed, she deduces the clothes below must belong to her husband.

"Have you completely lost it!" she screams. "Answer me, Ted!"

"I will answer you, but please do not call me 'Ted'," replies the toga-shrouded figure. "Ted Rumpkin is dead. I killed him."

"Great. Just great. What should I call you?"

"I haven't decided."

"Well, I have a suggestion. How about Mr. Moronic Freak!"

"You are angry, and I understand. But please realize your anger is for Ted Rumpkin not me."

Bambi has made her way downstairs to find Myron sitting on top of Cecil Leadman. Myron has Cecil's pistol and has the barrel pointed at Cecil's skull, a skull that possesses a growing contusion, compliments of Myron's boomerang.

"Who is that?" asks Bambi.

"We haven't been introduced," answers Myron.

"Who are you?" Bambi demands, but is answered only with a moan. "What are we going to do with him, Myron?"

"I haven't gotten that far."

smoke and gravity

"Well, I have an idea. I'll be right back." Bambi runs up the stairs and returns with the Dangler, which she secures from one of the high oak rafters of the living room. At gun point Myron forces Cecil to don the apparatus.

Once they have Cecil dangling from the ceiling, Bambi finds a roll of duct tape in the garage and wraps Cecil's hands together with abundant layers of the gray tape. Then she does the same to his feet.

Confident that the prisoner is secure, Myron pours himself a gin and tonic.

"Should we call the cops?" Bambi asks.

"I don't know. You know how I feel about cops." Myron sips his cocktail.

"What are we supposed to do then?"

"I've got an idea," says Myron.

"What is it?"

"What do you say we go upstairs and make love on the pool table?"

Bambi likes the idea.

"Damn it, Ted! You're ruining this vacation."

"Ted's dead."

"Stop it. Just stop it," Sissy demands. "You stand up this instant, and go downstairs and get your clothes."

"Those aren't my clothes. They belong to Ted... Ted's dead."

As Myron and Bambi admire each other's combinations and bank shots, Cecil Leadman struggles desperately to free himself from The Dangler.

He has found that if he jumps high into the air and then curls his feet and legs beneath him, he can send himself bouncing up and down like a human paddleball. When Cecil was a child, he had few friends. Actually, he had no friends, and he developed quite a talent as a paddle baller. His personal record was seven hundred seventy-seven consecutive strikes of the rubber ball with the smooth wooden handle.

Every paddleball set he'd ever had in his youth had one thing in common. Eventually the rubber band attaching the ball and paddle would break. Now that he himself is a paddleball, he hopes that trend will continue.

Up and down he bounces. Up and down and up and down.

Myron and Bambi continue to play on the pool table. Up and down they go. Up and down and up and down.

smoke and gravity

"Well, guess what, Mr. I'm-Not-Ted? If Ted Rumpkin no longer exists, then I guess I'm no longer his wife. Sissy Rumpkin is dead, too," Sissy says.

(We will honor this pronouncement by referring to Sissy from here on out as Tildy or Matilda.)

Tildy exits the hotel and rummages through the clothes scattered on the sidewalk until she finds the slacks containing Ted's wallet. She drops the wallet in her purse, crosses the street to Hyde Park, finds a large tree, sits under it, and cries.

Cecil Leadman's brain has become scrambled. The contusion on his skull has screamed with each of the seven hundred and seventy seven bounces. His legs have become as rubbery as the bands of The Dangler, but just as they give out, so does The Dangler.

With a sudden snap, the bands break and Cecil falls to the floor.

His scrambled brain and adjoined feet send Cecil and his duct-taped arms and legs in a tumbling circle around the living room.

One of the nice things about a scrambled brain is

that it has the ability to make things seem better than they are. Cecil's scrambled brain congratulates him on his freedom.

Myron and Bambi lie exhausted on the pool table.

"I've seen some pool sharks in my day," says Myron, "but I ain't ever seen anybody work a table like you."

Bambi smiles. "You're not too bad with the old cue yourself." She rolls to kiss Myron's chest, but as she is nudging his beard out of the way with her nose, a series of thuds travels up from downstairs.

Myron and Bambi race to the living room to find their prisoner circling around the room in desperate hops.

When Cecil Leadman sees the naked couple, his scrambled brain tells his legs to attempt to jump the coffee table and head for the door.

The plan fails from the start. Cecil doesn't clear the coffee table, catching his toes on the edge and plummeting to the floor, and since his hands are taped behind his back, Cecil is forced to break his fall with his nose.

Bambi goes to the kitchen for ice.

Once Cecil's bleeding and swelling have stopped, Myron decides they could all use a little relaxation. Bambi and Myron carry Cecil up the stairs, and the three of them are joined by Stonewall and Lee in the hot tub.

The person formerly known as Ted Rumpkin III — perhaps we could refer to him as TPFKT3 — dances around his hotel room in a state of bliss. He displays the grace of a Sasquatch ballerina.

The dancing sends all thoughts of his old life flying from his mind. The very last part of his old brain has this thought on its way out: Damn it. I wish I could at least remember what Linda Coxdale's breasts felt like.

The thought going through Cecil Leadman's mind is this: Germs. Germs. Germs. Germs. Germs.

Dog hair bubbles all around him. He can smell his bearded captor across the hot tub. Who knows what kind of germs that guy is sending his way? And the woman! The thought of being connected to a living vagina by several gallons of hot water causes his limbs to go numb. He must get out of the tub, but all his scrambled brain can tell him is this: At least the filth is distracting me from the pain.

TPFKT3 pirouettes and then collapses onto the bed in maniacal laughter.

Across the street in Hyde Park, Tildy Rumpkin continues to cry.

Myron leans back and closes his eyes as he enjoys the sensation of Bambi's soft hand stroking his penis. "This is the life, ain't it, my friend?" he says to the prisoner, but Cecil does not answer. Cecil, too, has his eyes closed. He forces his scrambled brain to create the image of himself surrounded in a Lysol-filled bubble floating through space.

Bambi's right hand works away at Myron's pleasure, but the rest of her is occupied with thoughts of how she can improve The Dangler. It's one thing for the bands to break on a house thief, but she can't stand the thought of them giving out on one of her future customers.

Eventually his imaginary Lysol bubble bursts, and Cecil Leadman plunges back towards Earth. He opens his eyes hoping to find that the last several hours have only been a dream, but even his scrambled brain cannot comfort him when he looks through the bubble-filled water, through the dog hair, through the millions of invisible germs, to see the woman's hand moving up and down her partner's cock. Cecil detects a smile through the man's beard, a smile that can mean only one thing; within minutes the tub will be filled with thousands of the stranger's spermatozoa. The moment Cecil's mind makes this realization, it shuts itself off and Cecil becomes unconscious, sliding slowly toward the bottom of the hot tub.

Myron is focused on his cock and does not notice Cecil's submersion. Bambi is busy mentally improving The Dangler and does not notice either. Stonewall and Lee notice, but it is obvious to them that Cecil Leadman is not a dog person, so they say nothing.

Duke takes his seven hundredth step since being forced to restart his count after hearing that the pearl of life is a pair of breasts. This seven hundredth step brings him to the fringe of Hyde Park.

He is delighted that a cloud-filled sky has cast a grayness over the park. The gray seems to pull the green from the oaks, intensifying the earth tones of the trunks, as well. He wishes the messenger had said, "Grayness is the center of life."

As if the goddess has heard his wish, one of the trees begins to speak to him.

Back in the hot tub, Myron tries to make conversation. "This is the life, ain't it, my friend. Nothing like being in a hot tub with a couple of friends and two beautiful dogs. By the way, what's your name?" Since Cecil Leadman remains submerged, there is obviously no reply.

"Come on now. We're either going to hand you over to the cops, or we're not. No use holding out on your name."

Still no reply.

Myron lifts his head to give his prisoner a friendly smile, but when he opens his eyes, he scolds himself for being careless. The prisoner has escaped.

"Quick, Bambi. He's getting away."

Myron and Bambi spring from the tub and run out of the room.

Tiny bubbles leak from Cecil's lips, flying to the surface of the tub where they become lost in the crowd.

The Oak Goddess is speaking to Duke. With her magic she has recreated the wails of the woman from Harrods through the voice of the tree in front of him.

Now there is no doubt. On this, his seven hundredth seventy-seventh step since seeing the woman, the Oak Goddess has called to him to verify that the woman had been a messenger. An angel. His angel. Relieved at the possibility of being able to ask more questions, he falls to his knees, bows in awe, and joins the oak in tears.

Crying brings clarity to Tildy. The tears point out that she, too, can walk away from the Rumpkin farce. Life awaits her.

Maybe her life will be one of solitude. Maybe she'll find another man. She is certain of one thing: No more idiots. She removes her driver's license from her wallet and addresses the picture. "You are free, Tildy Rumpkin. And remember, no more idiots." She rises to her feet and leaves the arms of the large oak. She will go to the airport and board a plane for America. There, she will get her car and leave forever the man who has already left himself.

No more idiots, she repeats to herself. No more idiots. Especially like that one, she thinks, as she spies a tearful man bowing to the oak she has just left.

Perhaps it is this man's crying that distracts Tildy and keeps her from noticing that she has left her wallet and room key under the oak.

Myron and Bambi give up the search, convinced Cecil Leadman is no longer in the house.

"Back to the hot tub?" suggests Myron.

Bambi nods. "Sounds good to me."

Eventually Duke notices that the tree has stopped crying. He opens his eyes and stares up at the broad expanse of branches.

"What do I do now?" he asks softly, but the tree does not reply.

He repeats the question.

Still no reply.

He moves closer to the tree in case the goddess is whispering. As he approaches he thinks he hears chimes, but looking down he realizes he has kicked a key, probably a magic key. Beside it is a wallet. Perhaps it is magic, too.

"Oh my God!" screams Bambi.

Myron comes running. "What is it?"

He enters the master bedroom to find Bambi pulling Cecil Leadman's limp body from the hot tub.

Bambi presses her fists into Cecil's abdomen, forcing a stream of water from his mouth. Several minutes of mouth-to-mouth revive Cecil's breathing, but he remains in a catatonic state, not even moving his eyelids to blink. Thoughts of dirt and germs have caused the gears of his mind to seize.

"Myron, what are we going to do?"

"I'm going to have a cigar," says Myron, selecting a stogie from the humidor beside the bed.

Duke runs at full sprint to the Travilly Hotel, counting as quickly as he can to keep track of his steps.

He is out of breath and trembling as he knocks on the door of room 777. The door is answered by one of the Goddess's attendants. He is a middle-aged sprite wearing a loose fitting toga.

TPFKT3 dances to open the door. On the other side he finds a panting man who between gasps of air says, "The Goddess has sent me to find this woman."

TPFKT3 takes the driver's license from the man and examines it.

"I'm sorry. This woman no longer exists," he tells the stranger, shutting the door and dancing back across the room.

Duke is becoming frustrated with the Oak Goddess. So far she has sent him a worthless message and a dead messenger.

Or maybe it does make sense. Maybe the Oak Goddess used the body of a woman freshly dead to be a vehicle for her message. Yes, that makes sense. But still, "Two damn breasts" is not much to go on. But then again, how many people ever get to have any contact with the Goddess at all? Duke decides to consider himself fortunate.

Not knowing what else to do, he proclaims to the surrounding sidewalk traffic, "It is on this day that I truly begin to walk!"

Following this simple announcement he strides off.

Left, right, three, four, five...

Myron and Bambi have propped their prisoner on the couch and have been staring at him for nearly an hour. His breathing remains strong, but he continues to stare away, completely motionless. Myron puffs on his cigar. He blows smoke in the prisoner's face, but the catatonic man does not blink.

Is it coincidence that the person formerly known as Ted Rumpkin leaves his hotel, walks down the sidewalk to the precise slab of concrete from which Duke has just declared his rebirth, and makes this announcement: "All who hear my words, let it be known that Ted Rumpkin no longer exists"?

And is it merely coincidence that after publicly renouncing his name, the person formerly known as Ted Rumpkin takes exactly seven hundred and seventy-seven steps before coming upon his first idea for a new name? Is it merely coincidence that the name that springs to mind is "Elon," the Hebrew word for oak?

Yes, it is probably coincidence.

With Tildy trying to arrange a flight back to the states, Duke counting his steps, TPFKT3 searching for a name, Cecil Leadman stuck in a catatonic state, and Myron and Bambi watching Cecil be stuck, the most interesting participant in this story becomes the cigar butt that Myron has thrown into the garage.

Let's trace its emotional state during the brief interval of flight from Myron's hand to its resting spot and present location:

As it left Myron's hand, the butt was in a state of ecstasy, the ecstasy that comes to any being believing itself to be absolutely free. The cigar butt, having no knowledge of the laws of combustion, believed itself to somehow be responsible for its liberation from the smoked portion of the stogie.

And as far as the butt was concerned, it was the one who flicked Myron away, not vice versa.

And from there, having no knowledge of the laws of gravity, it believed itself to be choosing a downward flight to the concrete below.

At this point, Myron ceased to be a witness to the life of the butt, for, having partial knowledge of the laws of combustion, when he saw the stub of his stogie strike the concrete, he was satisfied in regards to the question of fire safety and shut the door.

The butt congratulated itself for willing the door to close behind the body it had just flicked into the house, and having no knowledge of the laws of momentum, it now deemed itself strangely attracted to the far wall of the garage. As it skidded closer and reflected for a split second, it recognized the object of its desire to be a stunning cube of red plastic, by which it now rests.

The butt quickly decides that its feelings for the red cube are of such strength as to merit a permanent closeness. The butt believes it has freely chosen to move no farther.

The butt, having sufficient knowledge of neither itself specifically nor the history of cigars in general, finds it merely interesting that one of its poles still smolders.

The butt, being young, declares that it has found a place where it shall rest forever.

Someone is bound to have once said, "Besides the eternal folly of youth, nothing is permanent."

The container of gasoline by which the cigar butt smolders sits many years separated from its youth. Day by day, meaning has slipped from existence. It is, however, mildly amused by the questions that come from the young butt: "Have you always had that beautiful spout? May I look inside one day? Does my size suit you?"

"Is this tiny wad of tobacco for real?" the gas can asks itself.

"What are we going to do?" Bambi has decided that the answer to the situation is to repeat the question every half minute or so. Perhaps she no longer even hears the words. Perhaps the question has transformed into a soothing mantra, relegating the problem into spiritual oblivion.

Had Ted Rumpkin III never crossed paths with Linda Coxdale's breasts, we might find the story of the cigar butt and the gasoline can less interesting. For without the breast scandal, it is likely that the Rumpkins' wealth would have been maintained indefinitely, perhaps even growing exponentially to be passed on to Teds V and X, and maybe even C.

And if the Rumpkins had not watched their money dwindle, they would still employ the services of Harry's Lawn Care with which they first became acquainted through fliers Harry delivered door to door. "Call me. I'll cut your grass. 729-7932."

And if Harry were still under the employ of the Rumpkins, there might still be a spare can of gasoline in the Rumpkin garage, but it would most likely be full, since Harry would have probably supplied his own fuel, and even if he didn't, he most surely would not have left the Rumpkins a nearly empty can in the garage as Ted Rumpkin had done when he last mowed the yard.

And if the container were full rather than empty, it is likely that even if a smoldering stogie melted through the plastic container, the subsequent flow of gasoline would be sufficient to squelch the glow before any ignition had a chance to occur. For, as elder Ted Rumpkins have twice told youthful Ted Rumpkins, it's not the gas, but the fumes that'll get you.

Tildy still waits at the airport, TPFKT3 still searches for a name, Duke continues to walk, Cecil remains catatonic, and Myron and Bambi remain baffled.

Regardless of what might have been, our can is empty, or perhaps it would be more accurate to say that it is full of fumes.

The fumes are young like the cigar butt. They have expanded to the walls of the container and are under the impression they have chosen to desire liberation from the can.

Within seconds, the young fumes will be granted their liberation. A small hole will form less than an inch above the level of the scant liquid that remains in the can. Once the hole forms, the young fumes will make a rush for it, streaming out into open air for the first time. What glory! What salvation!

Our cast still waits, searches, walks, stares, and stares at the staring.

The salvation will be short-lived, of course, will not even last a moment, not even a micro-moment. Not even long enough for the young fumes to begin to think a self-congratulatory thought over what they think they have brought about.

Boom. We'll tell the world how brave they were.

At first, Bambi thinks that the prisoner's brain has imploded. "What are we going to do?" she asks reflexedly.

But Myron does not even respond with a comforting, mumbled, "I don't know."

For he is already in the garage.

The melted remnants of the gasoline container burn like a candle. Even more troubling is the bundle of rags that has ignited and now begins to share its flames with a collection of kites that hang on the wall above it.

Myron springs across the garage and clicks a wall-mounted switch, sending the large garage door creeping slowly upward. A bluster of wind dances through the garage.

Myron yanks one of the kites from the wall, darts out of the garage, and throws the kite on the driveway. As he leaps to perform a two-footed stomp on the conflagration, a surly swirl of wind snatches the kite from beneath him, beginning a game of cat and mouse around the yard which doesn't end until the flames finally die out on their own accord.

Back in the garage, Myron sees that victory will soon be out of reach. Something desperate must be done to turn the tide.

(Years from now, Myron will have this thought: Why did something desperate have to be done to turn the tide? And having had this thought, he will raise his shirt with pride, and Bambi will kiss his faint scar.)

Myron grabs every kite, rag, and piece of plastic that contains anything resembling a flame, forming a bundle of fire which he clutches to his chest, and once he is certain he has gathered all possible flames, he again runs out of the garage, this time making his way directly to the lawn where he dives headfirst into the grass, rolls into and out of a flower bed (The bed is actually flowerless, nothing having been planted in it since the Rumpkins' pre-breast days.) and then rolls three more times before examining a bundle of ashen scraps and assuring himself the fight is over. He has won.

Bambi runs to Myron and helps him to his feet.

Now we have waiting, searching, walking, staring, and hugging.

Bambi gives Myron a hug strengthened by countless hours of testing her exercise ideas. Even the ideas that have failed have provided Bambi with ample exercise. Consider the Eggserciser.

The Eggserciser was based on these two notions: 1) Even the strongest of brutes can't break an egg by pressing on it from the ends. 2) Even the puniest of us is certain we can break an egg by pressing on its ends.

Bambi stumbled upon the idea one night not long after she and Myron began seeing each other. She was soundly asleep after a night of lovemaking, but the idea came to her in a dream and sucked her right out of the bed. She believed she had cleared the number one obstacle in the fitness industry: motivation.

The Eggserciser would eliminate the need for

discipline and schedule following. With the Eggserciser, a minuscule dose of incredulity would lead to hours of attempted egg crushing.

By the time Myron made his way into the kitchen for morning coffee, Bambi had depleted the egg supplies of three convenience stores. Myron drank his coffee in a kitchen with a floor decorated by over two hundred yolks and shells.

Bambi realized it was going to be difficult to design a device that could hold the egg securely without contacting any part of the egg except the very ends.

A month later she gave up, but smiled whenever she glanced in the mirror at the shapely arms that had been formed at the expense of the local egg population.

Back to the hug:

It is a hug scented by the smell of burned beard hair and sweat, sweat which has dried in the strong breeze while leaving behind its primal odor. Other than flickering images of the fireball as exercise apparatus, Bambi focuses her entire being on the body of her love and hero, a body that only a few minutes ago seemed buried in flames. I could hold him like this forever, she thinks.

With her chin resting on Myron's shoulder she looks

down the street. She takes in the millions of dollars' worth of homes, the manicured lawns, and the expensive cars.

Bambi clings even more tightly to Myron. She is about to utter the words, "You are my mansion," when her eyes catch a flash of red fur at the end of the street. The fur makes a quick turn onto Oak Way and disappears.

After galloping for over an hour, Stonewall and Lee trot into a wooded, undeveloped lot for a breather.

"Goddamn, that was great."

"Never felt nothing like it."

"Hey, you smell that?"

"Sniff…sniff…Oh, no!"

"Oh, yes! We've got to go find that bitch."

"Damn it, Stonewall! This is no time to be thinking about women."

"Are you kidding? It's always time to be thinking about women."

"Not now, Stonewall. First thing we've got to do is get these collars off."

Myron and Bambi scour Pickett on the motorcycle, leaving Cecil Leadman in his catatonic state on the couch.

It is well after dark when they give up their search and return to the house to make "missing dog" posters.

Cecil remains motionless on the couch.

"Damn, I was hoping he might be gone," Myron says, handing Bambi a gin and tonic.

"Thanks, Sweetie," Bambi says, looking up from her first poster which reads:

> Please come back
> Stonewall and Lee.
> We love you.

"I thought they liked us, Myron."

"Of course they did, Sweetie."

"Then why'd they run away?"

"Maybe we showed them that they deserved a better life than what my sister and that moron can offer."

"I guess you're right," Bambi says. A smile spreads across her face as she begins the next poster. This one will read:

> Stonewall and Lee,
> Be cool.
> Have fun.

When the phone rings, Bambi is finishing her twelfth poster. This one reads:

> Stonewall and Lee,
> If you ever get
> the opportunity,
> you should check out
> New Orleans

Myron answers the phone, "Hello, you've reached the nut house; the nuts are out of town."

"Myron, hey, it's Sissy."

"You mean Matilda."

"Actually, yes. It's Matilda."

"Well, hi there, Tildy."

"How are things going at the house?"

"Hmm…I guess I'd have to say pretty damn exciting."

"Things have been exciting here, too. Too exciting actually. I just wanted to call and let you know I'm on my way home."

"What about your husband?"

"He's dead."

"Sorry to hear it."

"Well, I'm not."

"Myron, what are we going to do?" asks Bambi.

"About what?" Myron asks.

"About the garage. About the dogs. About everything."

"I guess things are a bit of a mess. But you know, that's the nature of life sometimes. In the end, it's all pretty much just smoke and gravity."

When Tildy walks through the door, this is what she sees:

On the couch, Myron and Bambi sit like bookends. Between them sits a ruffled looking stranger with mad, staring eyes. Across the stranger's lap rests a shotgun.

"Run, Tildy! He's crazy!" Myron exclaims.

"What is going on here?" she replies, as this hopeful thought runs through her head: It's all been a dream. Linda Coxdale's breasts. Her husband's abandonment of himself. It's all been a dream with this bizarre final scene.

"He's a maniac, Tildy. Some canine fanatic. He's let the dogs go. He said they should be free."

"Of course, they should. We should have set them free long ago," says Tildy, still clinging to the hope that it is all a dream. "And what do you want from us?" she asks the stranger.

"He'll only talk to me," Myron explains, leaning his ear to Cecil's mouth. "...mm-hmm...OK...no, no funny moves, I promise," Myron assures Cecil and then explains to his sister and Bambi that the first thing the gunman wants Myron to do is to tie up the two of them, one upstairs and one downstairs.

Tildy allows herself to be led upstairs. In the guest bathroom, Myron closes the lid on the toilet and tells Tildy to have a seat. "Don't worry. I have a plan," he tells his sister as he binds her to the toilet with large rubber bands.

When Myron returns to the living room he finds Bambi doing a split on the floor, grasping the toes of her left foot, and inhaling deeply.

Bambi exhales. "We can't keep her tied up," she says.

To which Myron replies, "Sure we can. It'll be good for her."

A Brief Note Concerning Myron's Behavior
Perhaps some of us are a bit troubled by Myron's treatment of his sister. Why is he being so mean? Hasn't Tildy had a rough enough day as it is?

Before we intervene, let's give the situation just a little longer to work itself out.

smoke and gravity

Myron and Bambi hear a scream from upstairs and Myron goes to check on his sister.

Tildy's legs have grown numb, and the toilet seat grows harder and harder with the passing minutes. The discomfort has convinced her that this is no dream.

"For God's sake, he almost shot me when he heard you scream," Myron says, entering the bathroom.

"Untie me now. You untie me this instant and go tell that man to get the hell out of my house. I should have known better than to leave you and that stupid woman alone in my house."

Myron feels his blood surge against his temples.

"Apologize right now."

"For what? The truth? Now untie me."

"I think I better not," Myron says, turning to leave the room.

"Myron, stop. I'm sorry. I didn't mean it. I'm scared. That's all. I'm sorry. Please untie me," Tildy begs.

"Okay. I'll untie you. But you have to promise to stay in here and not do anything foolish. I think I almost have him talked into letting us go. But we may have to give him some money first."

"Whatever he wants, just untie me, please."

Myron loosens the rubber strands and Tildy slides to the floor.

Myron returns to the living room where he and Bambi have a cocktail and play Scrabble while the catatonic Cecil watches over them with his unloaded shotgun.

"Sweetie, I'm not sure 'fundiddly' is a real word," Myron says.

"If it's not real, then I guess you won't mind when I say no more 'fundiddly' for you."

Myron concedes, and Bambi smiles as she points out that her "y" tile is on a triple word score.

After two more Scrabble games and several cocktails, Myron and Bambi are ready for sleep. Myron retrieves an armful of blankets from the closet and makes a pallet on the living room floor. Then he takes the smallest, thinnest blanket upstairs to his sister. "This is all he'd allow me to bring you," he explains to her.

Myron goes back downstairs and quickly falls asleep beside Bambi's warm, nude body, his head snuggled against her shoulder. As Myron sleeps, Bambi studies her belly. The rash left from Myron's industrial strength hand cleaner has almost disappeared, meaning she will be able to return to work at Heavenly Slice in a day or two.

At times, Bambi thinks Myron might be happier if she retired from the exotic dance trade, but he insists her dancing doesn't bother him, that whatever makes her happy makes him happy. Occasionally, Myron even goes to work with her, drinking gin and smiling as he watches the other men become nervous little boys as she sways in front of them. Some laugh self-consciously, while others stare in silent awe.

As Myron begins to snore softly in her ear, Bambi rubs her hand over her body and tries to understand how the sight of her flesh can possibly provoke such reactions from the male species. Once she understands this, she tells herself, she will give up dancing and concentrate full-time on her inventions. In the middle of this thought, Myron sighs. His sleeping mouth finds her breast and begins to suck gently on her nipple. Bambi shudders with delight and realizes there are some things she will never understand.

And where are Myron's thoughts at this moment? Perhaps they are many years away, suckling from another familiar breast. Perhaps he is being held by a young mother who cries as she feeds her newborn son.

On Christmas Day, 1957, Francie Fugate rose before dawn from another sleepless night, a night filled with nightmares of her husband's death offset by nursing and talking to her newborn son.

With tears running down her face, Francie opened her closet and reached to the top shelf to get down two of her daughter's Christmas presents, a small china tea set and a baby doll.

She placed the gifts under the large fir tree that swallowed up her living room. The tree and most of the other Christmas decorations, the candles in the windows, the manger scene on the hearth, and a large Santa stocking hanging from the mantle had been the work of the people of Pickett. Francie knew they had meant well, wanted to give Christmas to a family that had just lost husband and father, as if a holiday could distract in the slightest way from the house's sorrow. Francie appreciated their good intentions and was glad that Tildy would find a stocking and gifts under a tree, but she still could not help herself from wishing one of the candles would fall from its perch and make ashes of everything.

Back in her bedroom, Francie leaned over her son's crib and yearned for him to wake. She kissed him softly on the cheek. She stroked his sparse, almost invisibly fine, blonde hair. She kissed his cheek again. Still he did not wake.

Finally, Francie lifted her son from his sleep and held him tightly to her chest. The baby awoke, not with the opera-force wails his lungs so often produced, but with a soft cooing that warmed Francie's heart as she carried him to the living room and sat on the sofa, shutting her eyes to banish the fir tree and its clumps of tinsel from her sight.

As she held her son in the dark, she tried once

again to decide on a name. Henry. David. Paul. Phillip. James. Joshua. Matthew, Mark, and Luke. She ran through dozens of names, but none would stick; none came close to deserving the treasure she held in her arms.

Of course, there was one name that stood on the perimeter, waiting to be invited in, but she would not have it. Frank Fugate was alive in her soul, but she did not want her relationship with her son to be constantly infected with her yearnings and heartache for his father, just as she did not want the sacred memories of her husband being blurred by baby food and dirty diapers.

Francie pulled a breast from her nightshirt and offered it to her son who sucked greedily at her nipple as tears of sadness and joy fell from her eyes.

Tildy's four-year-old feet produced little noise as they made their way into the living room where she found herself unnoticed. This yielded a strange sensation for a young girl who had grown accustomed to rooms coming alive and radiating upon her entrance. "There's my princess," her father had always announced with open arms and an adoring smile.

So Tildy stood in the doorway, waiting for the world to catch up. As she watched her brother eat at her mother's bosom, she felt as if she might slip from the earth as nobody watched.

Three days earlier, Tildy had witnessed her father's coffin being lowered into a hole on the outskirts of the cemetery as the collection of mourners stared at her and whispered to one another with faces full of pity.

The following day she traveled to Charlotte to sit for hours as her mother talked to an attorney in a gray suit and glasses who looked as if he'd been placed on a rack and stretched several feet beyond his normal height, leaving his body as thin and scrawny as his toothpick-like arms. Tildy heard the man mention her father's name several times, giving her hope that her father had not been in the wooden box after all, that somehow he had been saved from the hole.

When Tildy and her mother left the man's office, they passed a small plastic igloo in which sat Santa. Santa was large, as tall as the attorney in the gray suit, but almost three times as thick. The man cried out a coarse "Ho-ho-ho!" that frightened Tildy, but did not keep her from dropping her mother's hand and running to the man's knee.

"Well, ho-ho-ho there, little girl," said Santa as he lifted Tildy into the air, his musty breath causing Tildy to turn her head as he placed her on his red velvet lap. "And have you been a good girl this year?"

Tildy shrugged her shoulders.

"Ho-ho-ho. I bet you've been very, very good. What would you like Santa to bring you?"

Tildy looked through Santa's damp breath and stared into his eyes. "I want my father to come home."

Francie heard her daughter's request and fought to hold back her tears, fought to keep her legs from collapsing beneath her.

"Well, well, now," stumbled Santa. "Would you like a doll? A pretty little girl like you needs a pretty doll to match."

"I just want my daddy," insisted Tildy.

"Well…I'll have to see what I can do," muttered the man from behind his cotton beard.

Francie grabbed her daughter from the man's lap. "Come on, Tildy, we need to get back home."

"In case Daddy comes?" Tildy asked hopefully.

"Daddy's not coming home," answered Francie, angry at the tears she could no longer restrain.

As Tildy waited unnoticed in the doorway on Christmas morning, she knew her mother had been right. The foul-breathed Santa had let her down.

Francie opened her eyes to find Tildy sitting beneath the tree, holding her new doll at arm's length and staring into its rubber face.

"Merry Christmas," Francie said, forcing a smile to her face. Tildy did not respond. "What a pretty doll Santa brought you."

Tildy dropped the doll and picked up one of the small cups of the china set, examining it with disappointment.

Francie took her breast from her son and tucked it into her nightshirt, her nipple sore, filled with welcomed and distracting pain.

"Looks like Santa knows what a good girl you've been," she said, moving to the floor and putting her free arm around her daughter.

Tildy freed herself from Francie's grasp, plugged in the lights, and searched again for her father behind the tree.

The rest of the morning was spent with Tildy reluctantly trying on new clothes: a blue plaid jumper, a red corduroy skirt with matching vest, a white cardigan sweater, and finally a white flannel night gown dotted with teddy bears and Francie remarking how pretty she looked in each new outfit.

By noon, Tildy's moping had lightened. "Mommy, can I take my dolly silly sledding?" she asked.

"Of course you can," Francie said. She placed her son in his crib and went to the kitchen where she found a short piece of rope amid a drawerful of Frank's tools. Francie shut the drawer quickly and pulled a skillet from the cabinet above the stove. She then tied the rope around the handle of the skillet and placed it on the floor.

Tildy set her doll on the skillet and pulled it tirelessly around the house, occasionally looking over her shoulder and calling, "Hold on tight, Princess."

Myron wakes his sister early in the morning. "The gunman said he wants you to cook breakfast for all of us," he informs her.

Tildy's body shakes with exhaustion, the hard, cold tiles of the bathroom floor having provided very little rest during the night. She is too tired to argue with her brother or the mad gunman, so she makes her way slowly down the stairs.

Their captor appears not to have moved since she last saw him, still motionless on the couch with the shotgun in his lap.

"So how do you want your eggs, Mr. Terrorist?" Tildy asks.

Myron walks over to Cecil and leans near his face. "He says he wants two, hardboiled... and he says to scramble two each for me, you, and Bambi... and he says some toast would be nice, too."

In the kitchen, Tildy fills a small saucepan with water and lets it drop heavily onto the front burner. Then she plucks two eggs from their carton and plops them into the water, causing several drops to spring out of the pot and sizzle on the burner.

She breaks six more eggs into a bowl, unconcerned with the chips of shell that join the yolks and whites. As she beats the eggs, Tildy begins to cry. She pours the contents into a cast iron frying pan and collapses to the floor.

Myron runs to the kitchen and finds his sister tugging at fistfuls of her hair. Tears are running down her face as she repeats over and over, "Why?…Why?…Why?"

It is the first time Myron has ever seen his sister cry. Guilt and pity move through him as he kneels to comfort her. When Myron places his arms around Tildy, he has this realization: This is the first time in many years I have touched my sister.

Sure, there have been numerous obligatory hugs, hugs that did little more than reinforce the lack of warmth between them, but now Myron feels not coldness, but a warm sadness as his sister wipes her tears on his shoulder.

As Myron comforts his sister, a taxi is pulling up in front of the Rumpkin house. When Duke Stubbins steps out, the first thing he notices is a mailbox overflowing with credit card bills, sweepstakes entry forms, and catalogs.

Hidden deep within the junk mail that presses on the walls of the mailbox is a single piece of handwritten mail. It is a letter to Ted Rumpkin from Linda Coxdale. On the envelope are three somewhat exotic stamps and an "AIR MAIL" label. If we get a chance later, perhaps we'll take a look inside.

"I'm sorry," Myron says, prepared to explain the entire ludicrous situation to his sister when the doorbell rings. Myron decides the truth can wait.

He goes to the front door and opens it to find an unshaven man with a duffel bag. He waits for the man to identify himself, but the man says nothing.

"May I help you?" Myron asks.

Duke Stubbins studies Myron's metallic eyes and long gray beard and decides he must be an immortal. "I don't know," Duke says slowly, his voice still a foreigner in his throat. "I am on a quest... Do you know this person?" he asks, handing Myron a wallet flung open to Tildy's driver's license.

"This isn't a good time," Myron says, putting the wallet in his pocket and shutting the door in Duke's face.

As the door swings closed, Duke Stubbins feels

swamped with defeat. With his head hung low he slowly begins the twenty-four pace journey back to the waiting cab.

He assures himself that he has tried his best, but in the end, the Goddess has rejected him. He will return to his silent life in Midford, to his daily hot dogs, to the familiarity of the Crossroads Tavern and Novella Lee's loving care. He will enjoy his quest, and he will always be appreciative for his brush with the divine.

But on his twenty-first step, Duke is distracted by a rapid tapping sound. He turns to the house and is overcome with delight at the sight of a familiar face. It is the Goddess's messenger knocking at the window.

She is shouting to him. He tries to read her lips and deciphers her message to be this: "Help!"

Help? Duke is ecstatic. The Goddess has decided to help him after all. He rushes back to the house, lets himself in, passes through the living room without noticing the shotgunned man on the sofa, and goes to the kitchen where he falls to the messenger's feet. "Thank you, Goddess, thank you," he praises from the floor.

"Who are you?" Myron and his sister demand in unison.

"My name is Duke. Duke Stubbins. You first came to me in London," he says to Tildy.

She recognizes him to be the strange man from

Harrods, and for the slightest moment she recalls the beautiful diamond that she had been denied, and during this moment a warmth comes over her, as if she has summoned those magical diamond rays from across the Atlantic. The rays speak to Tildy in a way no real diamond ever has. Passing through the core of her id, through the housing of her very soul, the rays spill splinters of the ancient energy that belongs not to the diamond, as Tildy now sees, but to the universe. As she looks into her half-carat solitaire which yesterday she had moved from her left to right hand, the rays convince her that the idea of owning a diamond is no less illusory than the idea of owning the sky, or the moon, or the stars, and with this realization she pulls the ring from her finger and tosses it carelessly over her shoulder as she erupts with laughter and a balloon of warmth builds at her center.

The warmth spreads across her tear-stained cheeks and becomes so palpable that it is passed on to Myron and Duke. Even in the next room, Bambi feels a wave of energy move through her.

Cecil Leadman's catatonic mind is also affected by the warmth and begins to wake from its slumber. The first movements are internal. The deepest regions of his mind begin organizing images of his childhood. They relive the many afternoons Cecil watched from his bedroom as the other neighborhood children played in the vacant lot across the street. Then the memory of his first theft—a handful of jellybeans from the neighborhood dime store—is evoked. The memories begin to speed up and overlap. As Cecil's mind replays his decision to withdraw from college—he found his fellow dorm mates completely lacking in hygiene—it also begins to send neural signals out to the rest of his body. As Cecil's mind again experiences the sight of a boomerang flying through the air, it orders a twitch of the nose. And then a blink. As Cecil recalls the filthy bath with the strange couple and the filthy dogs, a wild roar emerges from the bottom of his lungs and pulls him into full consciousness.

Myron and Tildy run into the living room followed by Duke. There they find Bambi with her back against the wall, trembling as Cecil stands in the middle of the room with the shotgun aimed at her chest.

"Don't anyone move," Cecil demands, moving the barrel of the gun from one person to the next.

"Now just take it easy," Myron says calmly, taking a step towards Cecil.

"Myron, don't," says Tildy, grabbing his arm. "Just do what he says."

Myron is touched by his sister's concern. "It's okay, Tildy. Everything's going to be just fine." He takes another step towards Cecil with the confidence of knowing the gun is unloaded.

Cecil Leadman, on the other hand, is not aware the gun is empty. He is not a violent man, violence requiring too much contact with other people, but as Myron approaches, Cecil replays the filthy weekend in his mind and his finger quivers on the trigger. "I'll shoot," he warns.

"Nobody's going to shoot anyone. Now just give me the gun," Myron says, reaching for the barrel, and as he does so, Cecil's mind goes into spasms as it studies the dirt beneath Myron's fingernails. One of these spasms is relayed to the muscles of Cecil's right forearm which causes it to contract, sending the stock of the shotgun crashing into Myron's jaw.

Myron drops to the floor, a patch of blood surfacing gradually through his beard.

Cecil Leadman is horrified. Why couldn't things have gone like they were supposed to, he asks himself. Why wasn't the house empty? Why had he spent the weekend dangling from the ceiling and nearly drowning in a hot tub? "Why?! Why?! Why?!" he shouts as Bambi cradles Myron's head in her lap and strokes his hair.

"Talk to me, Myron. Say something. Say anything." But Myron says nothing and Bambi is terrified. A broad smile grows beneath Myron's bloody beard, but is of little solace to Bambi as she begs him to wake up.

What is the source of Myron's smile? Is it merely an expression by default, the facial muscles having gone as limp as the rest of his body? No, behind the smile there is more. The blow has sent Myron to a happy place, an innocent place, between a dream and memory, and within this memory all pain has disappeared.

Myron inhales deeply, and as the air rushes in, it is thick with a sea-like aroma, full of salt and life. The smell is intoxicating. He brings his arm to his nostrils and the smell grows stronger. The smell is miles away from the scent of the Chantilly perfume his mother had worn throughout her life, yet as Myron inhales, he has no doubt that it is his mother that fills his nostrils.

And then the face of a man appears. The face is both familiar and strange. Gradually, Myron comes to recognize it as his father's face, not the black and white face of old photographs Myron spent his childhood trying to assimilate into a father, but rather a living face, made of flesh and immediately tangible. Myron cries out to his father and is rewarded with a twinkle from dark, loving eyes.

Myron reaches out for the beard-stubbled face, but as he extends his arms, he finds them to be no more than tiny limbs, and at the end of the tiny limbs are miniature, hairless versions of his hands.

His father responds, reaching out his own hand and

spreading it against the wall of glass that separates them.

"I love you, son," he hears his father say.

"And I love you," Myron attempts to say, but his tongue is small and clumsy and he can only let out a meaningless cry.

"I'm excited... and scared. I want the world to treat you well... All I will ever ask of you is to be a kind man. I want you to be a kind man. Treat people well... And I want you to love your sister and mother as much as I do," his father says.

Myron reaches out again, straining his chubby legs and arms and wiggling in an attempt to free himself from his blanket.

Another man appears and soon he and Myron's father disappear.

"I love you, Father," Myron calls after them as the glaring whiteness disappears and Myron is left alone, surrounded by darkness and his newborn thoughts.

Tildy has had enough. She points a long, thin finger at Cecil as if it, too, is a loaded gun. "I'm warning you, you, you Cro-Magnon thug. You leave this house this instant, or else!"

Cecil Leadman is tired and is in no mood for threats. "Or else what?" he sneers.

At this instant, Duke Stubbins realizes the truth of the situation. This scenario must be a test of his devotion to the Goddess, he assures himself.

"Or else you won't get this," he interrupts, raising his canvas duffel bag.

"And what would that be?" asks Cecil Leadman.

"It is my offering," Duke says solemnly.

"Your offering?"

Duke cautiously places the bag at Tildy's feet. "I only regret that my simple life gives me no more to offer in the name of the Goddess."

Tildy kneels and unzips the duffel bag. The first thing she pulls from the bag is a notebook, a ragged three-ring binder stuffed with yellowing pages that have several vertical lines drawn down them to form makeshift calendars. Each page contains dozens of squares with numbers in them. In the bottom corner of each page are two circled sums. "What is this?" asks Tildy

"It is my life's work," offers Duke, assuming that the goddess possesses omniscient powers and is fully aware of the importance of a lifetime of walking.

Tildy glances back down at the bag expecting to find more notebooks, but what she sees, instead, is cash. Lots and lots of cash. She grabs a bundle and thumbs through it. One hundred dollar bills. Another bundle more hundred dollar bills.

Tildy's materialism fights to free itself from the

influence of the diamond soul rays, but after a heated skirmish, diamond power prevails and Tildy tosses the duffle bag to Cecil.

Cecil is ordinarily quite repulsed by the filthiness of paper money, but after a quick calculation he comforts himself with the fact that the bag might contain as much as a quarter of a million dollars.

Meanwhile, Myron begins a groggy journey back to the present. He regains consciousness just in time to see Cecil run down the driveway, throw the shotgun into the front yard, and ride away in the cab in which Duke Stubbins had earlier arrived.

"Thank you, Goddess," Duke says as Tildy freshens his drink. Tildy rolls her eyes, but tells herself there are worse things one could be called. Tildy, Duke, Myron, and Bambi are playing Scrabble and recounting the week's events. Duke takes a sip of his drink and enjoys the tickling of the gin and tonic passing over his still rusty vocal chords.

"So, Mr. Duke Stubbins, how should I put this?" Myron begins as he leans over the Scrabble board to place his tiles for "serendipity," good for thirty-four points with a double word score. "Who in the hell are you, anyway?"

Everyone laughs except for Duke.

Who am I? Duke's spent years pondering the nature of life. He has studied the people of Midford, Ohio as if they lived in a huge ant farm, toiling and tunneling their way through life as he sat back and watched. If Myron had asked him about Ernie Paxton of Ernie's hotdogs or Molly Rendale from the Crossroads Tavern, he could fire away with his recently revived voice. But *Who is Duke Stubbins?* seems far beyond his grasp.

The group has paused, and their silence seems to be demanding an answer.

"I'm a wanderer," Duke says at last, embarrassed by the insufficiency of his answer.

"I'm a bit of a wonderer myself," Myron says, drawing his new letters from the bag of wooden tiles.

"Did you say 'wanderer' or 'wonderer'?" probes Tildy. Duke is impressed by what appears to be her genuine curiosity.

"I walk," Duke explains.

Tildy stares, still trying to understand.

"I dance," Bambi says in an attempt to make Duke feel more comfortable.

But Duke hears her comment as if it were a far away whisper, for his attention is captured by Tildy's gaze.

At first Duke is frightened. He isn't sure what is happening, but Tildy's stare seems to be melting something between them, some sort of wall, melting the boundary that exists between all of us as we scurry past each other chasing our busy lives. Duke wonders what the Oak Goddess is doing to him. As the wall melts, Duke feels his pulse rise as if he were panting toward the end of a long, rapid walk, his heart swelling up against his rib cage. This is the first time Duke has fallen in love.

As the wall melts further, Duke wonders if Tildy sees what he sees.

A flash of her eyes answers his question.

How do we describe what we are witnessing without delving into melodrama? Perhaps we should compare Duke and Tildy to two computers that suddenly find themselves connected by a mysterious cable that has plunged deep into their respective hard drives.

In a flash, large chunks of Tildy's life are downloaded into Duke's mind. He knows she has looked at another man the way she now looks at him. He knows she has never understood why that man, her father, had to leave her life.

And he knows Tildy loves her brother.

"Tildy is sorry she burned down your tree house, Myron," Duke proclaims.

"What was that?" Myron asks, a little startled.

"Your first tree house. Tildy is very sorry she burned it down."

Myron remembers himself as a ten year-old, one lanky arm clinging to the smooth limbs of the great maple in their backyard while the other lanky arm struggled to tug timber through the branches. He thought of the all the dreams he had dreamt as his rickety tree house swayed in the gentle breeze, of the deck of playing cards featuring topless women he had kept hidden in the secret compartment behind one of the walls where he also kept an old bowie knife that had belonged to his father and whatever cigarettes he and Scotty Sherring had managed to pilfer during the week.

And then Myron remembered the day he returned from Scotty's house to find that his tree house had been reduced to a pile of charred, smoldering lumber lying on the ground.

"It's true," confirmed Tildy. "I was so mad at you. Remember? It was the day you caught me using a pair of your socks to stuff my bra, and you teased me about it in front of Kathy Caswell. I was certain the whole school would find out." Tildy says, baffled by Duke's knowledge of the event, amused by how catastrophic Myron's divulgence of her bra-stuffing had seemed at the time. "As soon as you left, I went up to your room and got all of the socks out of your drawers. Then I took them up to your tree house. I almost fell and killed myself trying to get up there. Then I piled the socks on the floor. I realized I hadn't brought any matches, but I found a box up there and lit the pile of socks. As soon as I was back down on the ground, I realized it was a mistake, but I was too afraid to go back up. I cried all night after I saw how upset you were."

Tildy is saddened by the memory, but brightens when Myron points toward the smoke-blackened garage. "Maybe we can just call things even."

"It's a deal."

"But how did he know?" Myron asks, nodding in Duke's direction.

"I have no idea," Tildy says, smiling at Duke with nervous excitement as Bambi begins placing tiles on the board.

"I like it," says Myron, reading the word slowly because it's upside down ... "Harmony."

And now our story begins to wind to a close.

For the next four years, Cecil Leadman will consider himself a man on the run even though no one will ever contact the police about his break in. After all, is there any law against accepting an offering to the Goddess? Cecil spends these years sleeping in hotel rooms which he first lines with plastic garbage bags and then saturates with Lysol. When he finally decides that it's safe to stop running, he uses Duke's offering to purchase a couple of acres of desert property in Arizona on which he builds a large glass bubble house with one of the world's finest air filtration systems.

And is it merely a coincidence that on the same day that Cecil's bubble is completed, the man formerly known as Ted Rumpkin III finally decides on a name? For several months he's been seeing quite a bit of an aspiring young actress whom he met at auditions for a production of *A Comedy of Errors* by a small theatre company called The Misplaced Players. The actress's name cannot be verbalized, but is represented by the following symbol: ♋.

After much debate, the person formerly known as Ted Rumpkin III decides on a non-verbal name of his own. It is ☺.

And perhaps now we should take a minute or two to take a closer look at Linda Coxdale's letter to Ted Rumpkin/☺.

For the last four years the letter has resided in a box filled with other items that Tildy was saving should her ex-husband ever reclaim his old identity, but only yesterday she decided she had held onto the box long enough, and now it rests in the Pickett landfill; old diplomas, family photographs, a birth certificate, and a third place skeet-shooting trophy all beginning to take on the smell of sour milk.

smoke and gravity

As we open the envelope, out falls a picture of Linda standing behind a bone-thin child who stares into the camera with a wide smile and curious eyes.

```
Dear Dr. Rumpkin,
    I've wanted to write you for some
time and let you know that your money
has gone to good use. Three years ago
I came here to India and opened an
orphanage. The House of Love is home
to over forty Indian orphans such as
Gulzar who you see with me in the
photograph. I hope that you find much
satisfaction in knowing that thanks
to you these children are able to
dream every night on a full stomach
in a comfortable bed. This project
has given more meaning to my life
than I ever could have imagined.
Thanks for all you've done to make it
possible.
                            Sincerely,
                         Linda Coxdale


p.s. It appears I owe you a bit of an
apology. A few weeks ago during a
session with a Buddhist monk, I was
```

given total recall of every moment of
my life, and it seems it was my hand,
not yours, that fondled my breast
during the extraction. Funny how
things work, isn't it? Take care and
thanks again.

And what about the rest of our cast? If we go to Pickett, we find Novella Lee, sitting in a large, wooden rocking chair the only piece of furniture she brought along in her move from Midford on the spacious deck Duke and Myron built right after they finished adding two bedrooms and another bathroom onto Myron's house.

Novella Lee has in her lap a calculator and several accounting reports for Dangler Enterprises which has become the ninth largest manufacturer of exercise equipment in North America.

At Novella Lee's feet, two graying Irish Setters are deep in conversation.

"... then there was the week in Key West; that was a helluva time, wasn't it, Stonewall?"

"You can say that again. We've had ourselves some fun, haven't we?"

"You've got that right," Lee says as he rises and arches his back in a yawning stretch, recalling the scent of an adventurous mutt with whom he'd had a two week affair in Miami. "Let's go see what's for dinner."

In the kitchen, Tildy tosses Stonewall and Lee two fatty scraps of steak as Bambi peers out the window at Myron and Duke in the backyard.

"You know," says Bambi, "I didn't think you'd ever convince Duke that you weren't the Oak Goddess."

"I'm still not sure that he's completely ruled out the possibility," laughs Tildy, opening the door to announce dinner.

"We'll be up in a few minutes!" Myron shouts, pulling a small orange boomerang from the laundry bag and handing it to Duke.

"It's no use, Myron; I'll never get it." Duke takes the bourbon bottle from his tool belt—a birthday present from Myron and Bambi—and freshens his drink.

"Of course you will," argues Myron. "You just need to put more wrist action into it."

"More wrist. Less wrist. Into the wind. Away from the wind. There's just too much to get straight."

"Come on, one more throw," Myron protests. "Just reach back and hurl it."

Duke takes the boomerang and clips his drink into the tool belt. "More wrist?"

"More wrist," Myron nods.

Duke inhales deeply and heaves the boomerang into the evening sky, watching with amazement as it soars smoothly above a distant row of silhouetted trees, turns gradually to the left beneath a rising crescent moon, and then continues to circle back, hovering, waiting to be plucked from the air.

Book Club Reader's Guide

When master tree house builder Myron Fugate agrees to house-sit for his sister and her dentist husband, the unexpected becomes the norm. The Rumpkins barely have time to cross the Atlantic before Myron and his girlfriend Bambi capture Cecil Leadman, a compulsively clean house thief, and the hilarity heats up. Throw in two mischievous Irish setters, a wealthy mute traveler, and an appearance from the oak goddess, and the story begins to sprint towards its delightful resolution.

Beneath the abundant laughs, Neagle pays homage to all of us as we face a world that often makes little sense and leaves us longing for direction. What are we to do in a world devoid of reliable road maps? How are we to stay afloat above the chaos?

If Myron Fugate has anything to do with it, we kick back, enjoy the ride, and love as much as we can along the way.

1. What causes the sibling rivalry between Myron and Tildy? How is it resolved? Is sibling rivalry an inevitable part of growing up?

2. What do we know about Myron from his profession as a tree house builder?

3. When Sissy/Tildy asks Myron to give Bambi her love, Myron responds, "No, I won't give her your love. Besides if you finally found

some, you should keep it." What does this reveal about their relationship?

4. How important are Bambi's exercise inventions to plot development? To the development of her character?

5. In what ways do Myron and Bambi express their creativity? Does their creativity have a positive effect on each other? On other people? Is creativity evident in the behavior of other characters?

6. How does Cecil Leadman's obsession with cleanliness impact his life? In what ways is his behavior similar to Duke's?

7. Why does Duke Stubbins begin walking and counting his steps? What purpose does this serve for him? What makes it possible for him to stop?

8. What relationship does Duke have with his two fathers? What role does Novella Lee play in his life?

9. What does Francie mean when she asks Frank, "Where's home?" How does he interpret her question? What results from this misunderstanding?

10. Sissy's only thought as she returns to her London hotel is, "If I can't buy diamonds, I might as well be dead." What does this tell us about her value system? Does reverting to her childhood name shortly thereafter suggest a change in values?

11. Explain Myron's statement to Bambi: "Within each boomerang lies the great Tao, and if one can access the Tao and let it run through their body, through the soul, the result will be a perfect toss, and the boomerang will return to the thrower as easily as the seasons return to the earth." Why does this statement trigger Bambi's realization that she is falling in love with Myron?

12. Do the names of the characters reveal characteristics of their personalities? What is significant about Tildy's and Ted's name changes?

13. What is the role of luck or chance in the lives of the characters? Is luck, good or bad, an element we all encounter? Is luck the same as fate?

14. Linda Coxdale's letter to Ted Rumpkin, III confesses her error in accusing him of molesting her and thanks him for giving her the money to open an orphanage. She comments, "Funny how things work, isn't it?" To what

other events in the novel does this remark apply?

15. Why is this book called *Smoke and Gravity*? What qualities do smoke and gravity share? What is their effect on us?

16. *Smoke and Gravity* concludes with Duke's successful boomerang throw. What does this tell us about his growth during the novel? Is the same growth evident in other characters?

About the Author

A former tennis instructor, securities broker, barge driver, and tree surgeon, Win Neagle now lives in Raleigh, NC and teaches in the English Department at Louisburg College. While writing and teaching consume much of his energy, riding his vintage motorcycle and tossing boomerangs are two passions he shares with the protagonist of his first novel.

Printed in the United States
135329LV00001B/52/A